After Dinner Conversation Themes
Interpersonal Ethics Edition
Philosophy | Ethics Short Story Fiction

After Dinner Conversation *Themes* – Interpersonal Ethics

This magazine publishes fictional stories that explore ethical and philosophical questions in an informal manner. The purpose of these stories is to generate thoughtful discussion in an open and easily accessible manner.

ISBN# 979-8-9924170-3-6 (Print)
ISBN# 979-8-9924170-4-3 (Digital)

Library of Congress Control Number: 2025945131

Copyright © 2025 After Dinner Conversation®
Editor in Chief: *Kolby Granville*
Edition Editor: *Kate Bocassi*
Story Editor: *R.K.H. Ndong*
Copy Editor: *Kate Bocassi*
Cover Design: *After Dinner Conversation*
Design, layout, and discussion questions by After Dinner Conversation.

https://www.afterdinnerconversation.com

After Dinner Conversation is an award-winning independent nonprofit publisher. We believe in fostering meaningful discussions among friends, family, and students to enhance humanity through truth-seeking, reflection, and respectful debate. To achieve this, we publish philosophical and ethical short story fiction accompanied by discussion questions.

Table Of Contents

* * *

From the Edition Editor

One of my favorite parts of being human is that we're a social species. That when it comes down it, all we have in this world is the relationships with our friends, our family, our neighbors, our acquaintances and teachers and bus drivers and all the countless people that affect our lives in some way or another. And whom we affect right back.

We all hold a power in our hands in our hopelessly social society, a potential in every interpersonal interaction. The potential we have to love, to nurture, to lend a helping hand. The potential to harm, to abuse, to insult, to hate. And everything in between.

As a copy editor for this magazine, I've read a lot of wonderful stories, but there are always a few that really linger in my head for weeks, if not months. Out of those favorites of mine, I've curated this collection of interpersonal pieces. The authors of these stories interrogate the nature of relationships, the potential to help or harm, the rules and expectations and consequences of living in social society. I hope they stick with you as much as they did me, and that they make you reflect on that incredible power that we all have.

Kate Bocassi – Edition Editor

Corporate Head

Jacob Orlando

* * *

<u>**Content Disclosure**</u>: Explicit Sexual Content; BDSM Themes; Strong Language; Hate Speech; High Intensity

* * *

Look at you.

On your knees on the floor of your apartment under some guy you met by the bar less than an hour ago after you shared the last of your Manhattan and then left together, your tummy all tumbles, your muscles all mush, your tongue all wet. You stare up, snake charmed, as he sneers down at you.

Where do you belong? Here on your knees.

He's a total package. He's a grower and a shower. He slaps you hard, handles you heavy, presses your face to the floor, and laughs. You see the phone and hear the shutter fly, but you can't say squat. He's stuffed musty boxers down your throat.

You feel, deep down, the black no good.

* * *

Look at you.

Sat by the boss at the board retreat, no better than a lap dog, ready to slobber all over whatever he pulls out. He always keeps the members busy. He's got a way about people. Everyone hangs on every word he says. He could be an emperor. He could be a garbageman. He's got the body and the face and the manners to bend anyone he wants.

We've let Rebecca go, he tells them. She was out of control. We'll need a new COO.

You want that number two spot. You've been at the company twenty-seven years. Nearly three decades under Boss Man's thumb. Maybe now, at last, he'll see you. Not just as a lackey, but as a worthy second and even successor.

He's moved on already. He wants to forget Rebecca, to bury her name, to burn away the traces of her. He looks to the second-quarter goals. Showers to flowers. The forecast looks good.

He cues you.

"Sunny days ahead," you say, a rehearsed break as he aces the perfectly prepared speech. You start to clap. The others catch on. He beams around, one hand heavy on your shoulder.

* * *

Look at you.

Same guy. He came back for seconds. You served up just what he wanted. You're weak. He loves that. No need for a strong sense of self. That would just cause problems.

Guy steps back and looks you over. Your ass cheeks burn red. Your back blooms purple. Your knees are raw. You feel hot all through. You almost can't put a thought together, except that he enjoys you, gets off on your use, and makes you feel useful.

You say, "Thank you."

He laughs. He takes you by the neck and roughly pulls you up, and then you can't speak. You're busy. Your head buzzes. Your mouth feels numb. You're sloppy. He gags you good, opens your throat deep, floods your tongue. He breathes, "Good boy." You're almost happy.

He pushes you back and throws you to the ground, phone out, camera on you.

"Bark," he commands.

When you don't respond, he threatens a punch. You cower, and he repeats, "Bark."

Now, you bark.

* * *

Look at you.

Two coffees, one black, and a splash of creamer for Boss Man. He doesn't look up as you set the cup down and say, "Easy, they're super hot."

He surveys a hefty sheaf of papers, a red pen handy. He turns a page, reads on carefully, and makes a mark by a bulleted paragraph. Then he scoffs and throws the paper down. "Sales," he says. "They've got a month to catch up, or there'll be cuts. Deep cuts."

You don't ask whether he expects consumer trust to return after the mess Rebecca made on her way out. Of course, he'd say. Who cares about one loudmouth on the rag? You'd rather not argue about how many people would have read the *New Yorker* exposé.

He doesn't look at you, but out across the park that separates the splashy corporate headquarters from the warehouse where most of the company's work gets done. You'd started there at the cube farm. Boss Man had brought you over and promoted you up through the ranks. You owe whatever loyalty he demands of you now.

You have a seat across the desk and take a taste of coffee. You savor the heat so as not to scald yourself. He chooses just then to say, "By the way, you've got the job."

The words break over you smooth as a splash of cool water. You try not to choke on your half-swallow. You're not sure you can trust yourself. You'd wanted the job for so long that the prospect was a fantasy. Even as Rebecca left, you hadn't dared to hope. But here you are.

"Really?" you reply weakly. Then, aware that you can do better, you say, "Sorry, just—part of me always thought the job would go to someone else."

Boss Man glances up at you. You worry about the second thoughts that could puncture the trust he's placed on you. But he flashes the usual charm and says, "Nope, you're my guy."

There's a pause. A new world opens up ahead of you. The stakes now seem so heavy. They drop anchor around your neck. You should be over the moon. But you can't shake the sense that someone has made a grave error of judgment.

You muster your resolve and say, "Thank you."

Boss Man tuts, already back to the papers on the desk, and says, "Don't let me down."

* * *

Look at you.

Drunk on your own lonely, down four shots and three beers before a handsome guy takes the stool on your left. He's gray, or maybe mature would be a better word, and comes off gentle. He puts up for the next round. You dry heave all your scattered thoughts about the job, a huge step up, but so much more pressure, and you're not sure you're ready.

"Don't worry about all that now," he says as the bartender drops two more. He offers a cheers and adds, "Just celebrate."

Gray seems almost too sweet. Not exactly your type. But he wants you, drunk and dumpy as you are. When you get back to your apartment, he looks around and says, "Sweet place."

You make out on the couch. He's handsy. You love how he needs you. But he's not hard enough. Not edgy. Not angry. He asks you, "What do you want me to do? Does that feel okay? Are you all good?" You try not to answer.

After he's done, he says, "Congrats on the new job." And then, "You free Thursday?"

You can't guarantee a date. But he takes your number. You watch as he walks down the hall toward the elevator. He looks back and waves. You wave back, then shut the door. Part of you hopes he'll ghost.

* * *

Look at you.

Star of your own press release. Not that you're newsworthy. But your new job could be. You don't know who wrote the release, but they've framed you up as a company man. You never cared much for the company. You just got comfortable under Boss Man. He always wanted you, and you were always eager to serve. You'd felt envy for Rebecca. He wanted her more. But you always knew you could outlast her.

You hate the way the release makes you out as a hero. Of course, there's not one word about Rebecca, no attempt to acknowledge what she alleged as she left. There's a dance around all that, a gloss on you as the guy who stepped up at a tough moment.

The release also blows smoke up Boss Man's ass. He loves that, no doubt. He expects everyone to brownnose. And you've always been so happy to comply.

* * *

Look at you.

Your photo, there on the phone screen. Guy has the press release open on a browser tab. He reads out the lead paragraph, then laughs. He looks at the photo and says, "That's you."

Horror thrashes at your chest, trapped beneath your sternum, lodged between your lungs. You don't know how he found the release. You'd never shared your name. You also hadn't set a safe word or any rules. Not that Guy would have to respect whatever you'd agreed.

You can't move. Your hands are bound at your back, and you're gagged on old socks. You can't stand, or speak. And anyway, what would you say for yourself?

You should have known. You'd assumed that he was lowkey, that he'd be buttoned up about whatever happened between you. But you should have seen what would come. You should have been more careful. You should have put a stop to whatever part of you craved the abuse. You should have been man enough to strangle off that need, to freeze or burn or cut out that part of you. But you never could.

Guy snaps a photo. He shows you. He toggles back and forth between the formal photo from the release and the one of you there on the floor. He takes more, some close on your face. You groan and try to pull your hands free, but there's no hope. He laughs.

"Want me to send these to everyone at work?"

You can't answer properly, but you squeal out a protest.

"Was that a yes?"

He lets you groan through the socks some more before he pulls them out. Your jaw aches. Your tongue feels dry and rough. You try not to cough.

"Please don't," you say. "They don't know about me."

He scoffs and says, "Who cares about you?"

You repeat, "Please don't."

He looks around your apartment, then back at you, there on the floor. He crushes your arousal underfoot and says, "You're gonna pay."

* * *

Look at you.

You're a wreck. Your clothes are shabby. You need a shower. You've never come to work so out of sorts. You've barely slept. You haven't eaten. Whatever you try, you can't hold down. You haven't spoken to anyone at work, at the bar, or anywhere.

Four days ago, you took out a hundred grand, stuffed a duffel bag, and let Guy walk away. You'd pretended that that was all you had, that he'd cleaned you out. But you could afford more. You have stocks and secret accounts, and you could always sell your place. Not that you want to. But now that Guy knows where you're at, you'll never be safe.

The thought has started to haunt you. He knows where you sleep and where you work.

Gray texts. The alert shoots through you. You half expect every message to be a folder of photos sent to the whole board. But no, just Gray. He wonders whether you're down for tacos. You let your head fall hard to your desk.

* * *

Look at you.

Brought to tears on a second date by a softball. "How's the job?" Should be a slam dunk. Great, except for the guy who could expose me as a depraved freak! All good except for that! And before you can wrap your head around a real reply, the sobs come, and then tears, and then he stands up and comes around to rub your shoulders and tell you not to stress, that a new job can be a lot, but that you are clearly capable or you wouldn't have been offered the role at all.

Gray suggests you take the food to go. He walks you home. You try not to see yourself there on your knees on the floor. You try to let Gray take your thoughts anywhere else.

You fall asleep on the couch. He's under you. He doesn't move.

* * *

Look at you.

You really thought you were clear, that you were out of the woods, that you'd moved on? Three weeks. That's a speck. Three more dates? That's progress. You start to get comfortable. Gray may be a match. You worry some that he's too oatmeal, too cardboard, too sweater vest. But maybe you don't hate that.

Now, when an alert comes through, you almost expect to see some sweet note, maybe *Have a good day!* or *See you soon!* So when Guy reaches you at your work address, the message floods fresh fear through you.

The sender seems anonymous. A junk account. The message reads, *Your place, 10 p.m. Have more.*

Attached, a photo. From the back, dark and blurry. No face. Not yet.

* * *

Look at you.

On your knees on the floor of the elevator. He slaps you and says, "No shame, huh?"

You say, "No."

He laughs.

He'd come early. As soon as you'd opened the door, he'd asked, "Where's my money?" You'd led across to the elevator. He'd pushed you down as soon as the door had closed.

You start to stand up when the elevator reaches your floor, but he says, "No, you crawl."

So you crawl. You can't deny that part of you wants to just turn off your thoughts and do what you're told. An easy way to move through the world. From your knees, you feel free. But you hope no one comes down the hall. When you get to your place, you want to stand up, but you know he won't let you. Your cheeks burn as you open the door.

Guy gets down the hall to where the room opens up before he sees Gray, who stands coolly by the couch. He wheels around on you and says, "The fuck?"

You're on your feet. Guy takes on an attack stance. Gray steps toward Guy and says, "You're not gonna get off so easy now."

"The fuck you mean?" Guy says and then to you demands, "Who's he?"

You don't know what to say. You hadn't meant to spew the whole story to Gray. But once you'd started, there really had been no way to stop. He'd wanted to help you. And you need help.

"So who are you, exactly?" Gray says. He steps closer.

"Fuck you," Guy growls.

"Let me see your wallet."

Guy tells Gray, "Get fucked."

Gray says, "Don't tempt me."

Guy steps back. He looks at you, then the door past you. He looks back at Gray and says, "Fuck you, old ass faggot."

He turns and steps toward you. As soon as he breaks, Gray slams them both to the floor. They scuffle and claw at each other. You fear that Guy may come out on top. After a breath, Gray throws you a wallet pulled from Guy's pocket. Not a moment to lose, you snap a photo. Then you rush back to the front door and hurl the wallet toward the elevator.

Face screwed up, Guy shoves you to the wall as he barrels by and takes off down the hall. You don't stop to watch. You shut and bolt the door. You hear Guy come back. He hurls swears and slams the door so hard you worry he could break through.

You don't respond. After a few calm breaths, you check the peephole.

He's gone.

* * *

Look at you.

The new COO. That's the subject. There's no message. Just the attachments. Half a dozen photos, face and body. None from the same scene. Each tells a new story. Each adds a new layer of shame. Boss Man and other managers are cc'd.

You feel your throat close and your breath sputter. Should you just go now and never come back? Could you get to your car before anyone who'd gotten the message got to you? Would Boss Man let you ghost, or would he want a more formal goodbye?

But before you can make a move, Boss Man messages

you, *come see me.*

He's not far, but the walk feels endless. Everyone who looks at you seems repulsed. There's no way any of them have seen the photos. But you can't shake the sense they all know, that they all see you as lesser, a nonman, a freak.

"Some photos," Boss Man says after you close the door. He leans back, feet propped up on the desk. He looks you up and down. You don't react. You can't even move. You don't know what to say. You expect the ax any second. He looks between you and the screen on the desk, and you know he has the photos open. Your cheeks smolder. He repeats, "Some photos."

You take a shaky breath and say, "You'll need a letter?"

He glances sharply at you and says, "We're not gonna push you out over a few photos."

"But they're—"

"Look, tough luck," Boss Man says. "Be more careful, okay?"

You don't understand. Why hasn't he walked you already? Shouldn't your career be over about now? "You're not—"

"No homophobes here," he asserts. "And after Rebecca, we need someone who does what he's told."

He can't seem to look away from the screen. You wonder what secrets he's tucked away, and whether he wonders how far he could take you, how comfortably you'd do as you were told. You doubt that he'll ever respect you. Not that you demand respect.

When he looks at you now, you can't help but see yourself on your knees. You almost drop then and there before Boss Man's feet. You feel the need to say you're sorry. You want to show that you're grateful. You wonder whether now, at last, you can speak the same language, whether he'll understand you better when you're down where you belong.

He glances up at you and says, "That'll be all."

* * *

Look at you.

Scared to leave your place. Scared to stay home. Wherever you go, you'll never be safe. He knows too much. He's around every corner. He haunts you.

There's some good. Gray stops by. He drops off food. He takes you out. You say you're sorry over and over, and eventually he tells you to stop. He says he was happy to help. He's glad you took control before you sank deeper. You don't feel any control.

He asks whether you really want to do the stuff you let Guy do to you. Not to yuck your yum. But what's the appeal? You don't know how to reply. You'd always been ashamed. You'd always wanted to keep that part of you secret. You'd always thought that you were broken. But you can't deny how you feel. You want to be useful. You want to help guys get off. You want to forget yourself, step out of your day-to-day and feel real.

But you have to make a change.

So Gray. He's not your normal type. He's no sado-douchebag-manwhore. He's just a sweet guy who wants someone to take on dates, cuddle, and generally care about. And sure, maybe he also wants an easy blowjob on the regular. You can handle that.

And he knows you. He got the crash course. He doesn't push you down or try to take advantage. But he doesn't make you keep secrets. He lets you be real.

* * *

Look at you.

At lunch across from Boss Man as though work has just kept on as usual. He made excuses to the others who saw the photos. A target of further attacks from external saboteurs. What anyone does at home out of work hours should be that person's alone to reveal or keep to themself. He stuck out some neck for you. Now he's ready to move on.

But he can tell you're not. When you space out as he goes over the rough second-quarter numbers, he sets the papers down and snaps for your focus. He grumbles, "The photos?"

You shake your head and say, "Sorry."

Boss Man leans forward, elbows on the table, and asks, "You gonna sue?"

"What?" You aren't sure you heard properly.

"Sue the guy?" Boss Man says. "Pretty sure he broke the law."

Gray had asked whether you wanted to call the cops. But why would you trust them? Boss Man saw law enforcement through another lens. He'd seen so many guys get sued for less. Why shouldn't you work out your trauma through the courts?

"No," you reply. "No need."

He looks at you sternly and asks, "You know the guy?"

Yes and no. Thanks to the help from Gray, you have a photo, a name, an address. And thanks to a few sharp web searches, you know more. You know what schools he attended. You know where he works. You have work and personal phone numbers. You even know the names and address of Guy's parents. They're not far, out on the edge of town.

You repeat, "No need."

He lets out a terse breath. He seems frustrated. He knocks

back a long guzzle of beer, burps, and says, "Then forget the guy, okay?" He sets the glass on the table. As he starts to get up, he says, "Remember, you work for me." You stand up too. He steps close and puts a hand on your shoulder. You smell the beer as he purrs, "You take orders from me."

He smacks your ass.

* * *

Look at you.

Calmer than you've been for weeks. More collected. More sure of your next words, your next move. Gray has clocked the change. He says, "You seem better."

You're on the way home from a drag show. You'd never been before. Gray had been more than happy to change that. He squeezes your hand. You don't answer.

Better may be a stretch. But you're numb to the fear that the other shoe may drop, that any moment Guy could send Boss Man a trove of photos to lord over you. And honestly, maybe you want that. Part of you goes to work every day and plays at normal. Part of you would rather be on your knees. You've been torn apart for so long.

You don't tell Gray about your plans. You don't know how long you can last. You'll have to snap sooner or later. You've already sold your place. You're ready for whatever happens next. As for Gray, he'll be better off ghosted.

You try not to cry. Gray looks at you but doesn't say another word.

You want to blame Guy. He's the one who took all the photos. You want to blame Boss Man. He's the one who dragged you so far up the corporate ladder. But you're the one to blame. You've never been honest. You've never let yourself be free.

* * *

Look at you.

On your knees so easy now. Boss Man has pushed you down hard. He grabs your ass, squeezes, and says, "Bet you love that." He makes you take notes as he takes calls, bare feet up on the desk. After, he has you massage them. He leaves the door open as he uses the bathroom so you can hear the stream splash across the seat. Then he tells you to clean up.

And you do. You kneel there and use paper towels to soak up the splatter.

You know that anyone else would stand up for themselves. Rebecca left over just a few off-color remarks. You should put your foot down. But your head buzzes through the fever of your daydreams. At last, you don't have to keep the parts of yourself separate. When you serve Boss Man at work, you're not ashamed. You're proud of a job well done.

Your new role hasn't panned out as planned, nor has the second quarter. Sales have not rebounded. Boss Man has cuts on the way. You feel fresh envy for Rebecca. She saved herself. What's left for you to save?

But put another way, what have you got left to lose? Boss Man should have Guy over. Then you'd have no more secrets.

But Gray watches from the corner of the scene. You wonder what he would say to them, and to you. Would he tell *them* to be ashamed? Would he want you to take control?

* * *

Look at you.

Your breath comes hot under the pup mask you hardly ever wear. What looks adorable on those smooth, barely cherry-popped porn boys appears laughable on an overgrown man. But the collar feels sexy, as does the harness you bought for yourself years ago. The leather pops under a loose cropped tank top. You eat up teeny short shorts that fall way below the strap of your jock.

The normals up and down the street have never been so gagged. You approach the door at number seven and knock. You don't need to prepare. You know exactly what you came to do.

An older woman opens the door. She seems wary. You can tell from a glance that she's Guy's mother. She looks you up and down, clearly unhappy to see your type there on her porch. She holds the door only partly open and asks, "What do you want?"

"Hellooo," you croon. "Any chance your son's at home?"

She steps back as though you've aggressed her.

"He's not here," she says. "Why?"

"Just wanted to return these." You procure the used boxers Guy had stuffed down your throat on one of your early hookups. She glares at them, then at you. Her face speaks horrors. "He left these at my place."

You toss her the boxers, and she can't help but catch them.

You don't need another beat. You turn and strut to the car. You don't know much about Guy's mother. You don't know whether he's close to her. You don't know how hard you've hurt Guy here, whether you've even done any damage at all. But she, at least, has reflected a heavy dose of shame for you to savor.

When you look back, she hasn't moved. She seems shocked and maybe even nauseated. You wave and holler, for everyone else along the street, "He's such a stud, your boy!"

Then you peel off before she comes unstuck.

* * *

Look at you.

You don't even react when Boss Man turns the screen around and shows you the folder full of dozens of photos. There are recorded shots too, some ten or twenty seconds, some longer.

"He says he'll send them to everyone on staff unless we pay," Boss Man says. "You know we can't afford that."

He turns the screen back and scrolls. You stand there as he thumbs through your shame. He rubs down to the bulge beneath the desk. He glances up at you and says, "Better get to work."

You come around the desk close to where he's started to unbutton and kneel. He laughs, taps your cheek, and gestures for you to carry on.

He's smaller than you'd expected. He's musky and sweet. Boss Man shoves you down, desperate to choke you, but you have no trouble. He's really pretty small. He scrolls some more, and then you hear, "Bark."

Boss Man murmurs, "Oh fuck."

Guy repeats, "Bark."

You hear yourself bark.

Boss Man comes close. He holds your head down and bucks at your throat. He doesn't even touch your uvula. As he starts to spasm, you close your jaw hard and let your teeth tear through flesh to tender muscle. He screams. You taste blood. At last, you feel free.

God, look at you.

* * *

This story first appeared in the After Dinner Conversation—May 2025 issue.

Discussion Questions

1. What parts of the story are most surprising, shocking, or offensive to you? What, if anything, does that say about you? What would it say about others if they had different answers?
2. What do you think caused (*if anything*) the narrator to develop his sexual preferences? Can a well-adjusted person have these same sexual preferences?
3. Initially, it appears the narrator and Guy were in a consensual sexual relationship. Is the issue with their relationship only when Guy extorts money from the narrator?
4. Do you think the narrator and Gray can have a more normal, more loving relationship? What (*if anything*) may prevent that from happening?
5. If the narrator enjoys being sexually submissive, what is wrong with him being in a job and having a boss that requests this from him? Why did the narrator fight back at the end of the story if his boss was only doing to him what he was asking Guy to do earlier?

* * *

Eleven Things I Have Left Now That My Daughter Is Gone

Vickie Fang

* * *

<u>**Content Disclosure**</u>: Strong Language; Sexual Situations; Substance Addiction Themes

* * *

1. The Walk Down Wilkins

When she was a baby, I used to hold her in my arms and walk down the worst part of Baltimore, Wilkins Avenue. Warm feel of her up close to my chest, little patch of blond hair against my neck, I walked right by those other females, lying passed out on their front stoops or sitting on the curb waiting for their regulars. I thought: Let the corner boys ride their bikes. I thought: Let the old men drive that strip with their eyes all over me. There wasn't anything I was going to buy from the boys and nothing I was going to sell to those men either. I was holding my baby in front of the world like I was saying, "This is mine. This little Promise is mine. And she is better than all of you."

And what did the world think? I didn't even notice. We were our own little two-girl parade. Fat whore and fat baby—call us that—and both of us sailing down that street like a door had been thrown wide open and we could go anywhere we wanted.

Those days and that feeling didn't last. Of course they didn't. But I let myself think they would. I never even left Wilkins, but when I walked with Promise, the clouds rolled over us like the first day of creation, and I really believed that my life had started all over again.

* * *

2. Five Clean Years

Five years go by: no dope, no whoring, no anything but keeping my baby safe. Her lying up in bed with me at night, me right beside her. But outside? A whole parade of cars with their lights crawling up the wall and across the ceiling. Nonstop men driving in from the county looking for women, especially the White ones. I'd lie there for hours, thinking about what they wanted and ask myself the same question: Out of all the sad things in the world, what was the worst—to go out to that street and get back in those cars, or to lie there in the dark, remembering?

One time Promise woke up and asked me what the lights were, and I said they were the stars. I said they crossed the sky above us, and we didn't care because we were like fish in the sea. And for a long time after that, when she got under the blankets, she wiggled like she thought a fish would, pointed her baby hand up, and said, "Stars." It was funny to her.

Promise'd laugh at the lights, and I'd stare into the dark and see my mother. She'd say, "Be good girls." My sister and I were eight and nine years old, but we knew we had to lay down. She watched for that—then she left and the men came in. My sister was in a bed beside mine, not looking at me, not talking. Not saying anything about what happened in that room afterward either because when men climb on top of you like that, you turn into dead girls.

Sometimes the men would be late, and I would start to hope they weren't coming, make believe that my mother said she didn't want their money anymore. Maybe my sister was hoping, too, but Mother never did send the men away from us, not one time. It's when you're clean and lying in your own bed with your baby that you remember what your mother did to you. It might be worse than going back out there and getting in cars again to lie there in the dark and think about how it all got started.

So all those nights were not the good thing I wanted them to be because Promise was a child asleep, and I was a woman caught on a train I could never get off of. That was the kind of daughter she was to me. That was the kind of mother I was to her.

* * *

3. As the World Turns

And the best times were when I was not using so much, so I was home and awake when Promise came back from kindergarten or first grade. I'd be watching *As the World Turns* with the Sunbeam bread and Welch's grape jelly all ready. She'd climb up on the sofa with me, and the two of us would go to

Oakfield together with Lily and Holden. We'd eat so many jelly sandwiches we'd be too full for dinner.

A couple of times, prostitutes with big hair and feather boas came on those shows. Those bitches were the strangest thing on TV, all of them so proud of themselves, talking tough. They wisecracked with everybody, even the police. What would women like that think of me, going on my dates wearing sweatpants and an old sweater, not knowing any special words at all, just mumbling the same things I heard my mother say?

What would Promise think?

The days got too long when she was in school, and all I could do was sit at home and remember old times. Even getting in the cars again was better than that.

* * *

4. Letter from School

"I had a big day today!" That was my Promise talking on a dead cell phone. I'd found it in a lot off North Washington one night and gave it to her for a toy.

"I got a letter." She wasn't looking at me when she said that. She was off in her own world—like usual when she got home from school. I was lying down on the sofa with my eyes closed, but I knew what she was doing. She was squatting in the corner near the radiator, rooting around in her backpack. "The important part is right here. Promise A. Lewis, the third grade. OLSAT test of Mental Maturity."

I opened my eyes and looked at her when I heard that.

"On a scale of one to nine, score nine!"

My score when I was her age.

"That means I'm smart."

The school called when I got my nine, and my mother shook me when she got off the phone. My head was bouncing off the wall, and she was saying, "I'm not going down there for any goddamned conference!" I never did find out what they wanted to talk to her about, and it wasn't until I was grown up that I realized she was afraid the school would find out about those men.

"Don't worry," I told Promise. "Your mommy will go to the conference," but I put my hand up over some pick marks on my face when I said it. I was using hard by then and getting into cars when she was home too. Promise didn't answer. She didn't like me to interrupt when she was talking on her phone.

"And I have another grand announcement to make," she said. "I, Promise A. Lewis, have been accepted to the Superior Learners Program." And that's when she put her phone down and looked at me for once. "I'm going to a new school, Mom!"

So that's what the school wanted to talk to my mother about—sending me somewhere superior.

"I want to go too!" I said. First thing out of my mouth; I don't know why I said it. "I want to go to that school."

And she was grinning, saying, no, no parents allowed. And I told her why not? I got the same score when I was her age, and I probably would have gotten to go to that school if my mother had let me, and Promise shook her head and said no I couldn't. No way. She smiled like the whole idea of me being smart too was some kind of a joke. That hurt me a little bit, but I didn't let her know. I walked over and leaned down, fixing her sweater for her, where she had it buttoned wrong. "Did you go around all day looking like that?" I asked her.

She just shrugged.

I said, "Better be careful in that new school. You walk around looking like that, and everybody's going to say, 'Look at that stupid girl. There goes stupid old Promise.'" I think I sang it a little. "Stupid old Promise."

She turned all the way around then and leaned forward so the top of her head was against the radiator, and I knew she wasn't going to say another word to me, not anytime soon. The way she was squatting on that patch of old brown carpet and wrapping her arms around her shins, she looked like a little bird, hunched over in winter. I rubbed her back for a while, felt the bumps on her spine. "Anyway, one of us gets to go," I told her. Finally, she nodded her head a little bit, yes.

* * *

5. It's Academic Superbowl

Almost midnight walking back to Wilkins. Promise in the fifth grade by then, but holding my hand the whole way.

"You scared?"

"No, Mommy."

Streets getting dirtier, plastic bags in the trees, broken glass. Cars coming in from Essex, Dundalk, anywhere else people want women and dope.

After a while, I said, "It's different in Harbor East."

"Yeah, better."

"Why do they call it Harbor East? What's wrong with East Harbor?"

"Sounds fancier."

"You like that? Those big townhouses? All that... all that fancy shit at the It's Academic meeting?"

Looked me right in the eye. "Yep."

We'd got to where the corner boys were making long, slow circles on their bikes. "Charm City." You could hear them calling it out. "Charm City." And then, "Girl." Charm City was what they were calling pot this week. Girl was heroin. I touched the ten-dollar bill folded in my pocket, realized Promise was watching me while I watched them.

"You going to win at the Academic Superbowl?"

"Impossible to say."

"First time *you* ever had any trouble saying anything."

Four or five men leaning against Martini's wall, smoking, watching. Soon I'd get her home, come back out again.

"I can get a ride."

"What?"

"You don't have to take me to any more parents' meetings. It's too far from the bus stop, and I don't need you there anyway."

I didn't say anything for a minute. Felt the coldness start seeping down my spine while I thought about what I looked like to those other kids and their parents. Eyes a little bloodshot, maybe. Was I scratching? Smoke enough crack and you're always scratching yourself. Everybody else dressed up so nice and poor Promise stuck with me. "You don't want me to come to any more parents' meetings?"

She shook her head.

"Maybe you don't even want me around at your old Superbowl either."

"You never come to anything anyway."

"Liar. I came all the way to Harbor East tonight."

"Cause the coach finally called you! You never came to one single meet this whole goddamned year."

But it was something for school—nobody told me parents were supposed to come.

That's what I wanted to say.

Or else, *When did you start hating me?*

Most of all, *Gonna beat your ass if you cuss at me again!*

What I did say was, "If you're so smart, I guess you don't need me anyway."

And she said, "Maybe not."

I couldn't look at her, just stared out at the street. Then I swallowed all my hurt and put my hand on her shoulder. "It's okay, baby girl. I don't need to go; I already know you're going to win." At least, I hope that's what I did. Some things are too hard to remember.

Anyway, I was back on the corner five minutes after I got her home. And a minute after that, I was in a little crowd behind a tall wood fence, one of the boys putting a crack pipe in my hand. That part of town, Black, White, it didn't matter—we all knew how to do it up. And when I told them my girl was about to win a national contest, everybody said they were proud of me.

* * *

6. Gummy Bear Momma

But we had good times too. My Promise loved candy, and I always tried to get her some no matter what. I was dope sick one time, so bad my hands were shaking and my stomach was like a bucket of wet mud, and still all I could think about was how I hadn't seen Promise for a week. I asked the drug man if I could pay $8.50 instead of ten so I could get my child some gummy bears. I was so sick I was stuttering, and people laughed when they heard me beg.

I don't know why, but I thought about her, and I left the line and bought the gummy bears instead. I ran back to Promise and watched her light up like a Christmas tree when I put those bears in her hand. Maybe she thought her momma had forgot about her, and there I was, giving her candy.

"Love you, Mommy!"

"Love you, Promise!" And then I got back out of there as fast as I could. I was heaving when I grabbed old Jimmy Mitchell, cane and all, and gave him a hand job for three dollars against the fence on Harmison so I could buy my dope.

I was lucky. The line had broken up while I was gone, but it got started again. I had vomit starting up in my throat, but there were people actually clapping when they saw me come back. Somebody even called me "Gummy Bear Momma." You have to have your own child to know why I wanted to cry right then, I felt so good.

And for a long time afterward, whenever I felt bad, I used to ask Promise, "Who buys you the gummy bears?" and she would say, "My momma does." That is one thing I will always remember.

* * *

7. No Respect

My mother slapped me when I was nearly thirty years old. Slapped my face twice right in front of Martini's with a bunch of men watching. And the guys were yelling out, "Oh god *damn*!" and "Take it easy, momma, that's your girl!" But you know they were all poking each other and laughing, too, especially when she called me a dumb-bitch-whore, and I started crying and saying I was sorry like I was a little kid again.

She and my sister were keeping Promise because I didn't have anywhere to live. My mother'd gone all the way down to Pratt Street and searched the abandonminiums—junkies, rats, rotten floors, and all—looking for me. Soon as she saw me: "Promise told me to go to hell! What are you going to do about her? She cussed her own grandmother."

And me: "Well, what did you do to her? What did you do to make my girl cuss you?"

That's when she hit me, and we both started screaming, but she could always scream louder than I could, and could always scare me too. "That girl's got no respect!" my mother screamed at me. "Nobody can stop her!"

I was still crying and wiping snot off my face, but when she said that about Promise, I stopped and stared. And I saw that the woman who used to be the most powerful person in the world wasn't so strong anymore. She was skinny and old, hardly able to walk her hip was so bad, and she was screaming because she was afraid. My mother was afraid of my child.

And I guess she knew what I was thinking almost as soon as I did because when she saw the way I was staring at her, she turned around fast and left. She looked like some kind of animal, an old rat staggering along on its hind legs, trying to find her way down that sad, ugly street with no idea of what was going on.

I would have followed her if I could have. I would have followed her the rest of my life with my arms around her and never let go, but she didn't want me. And I knew my own daughter wouldn't so much as cross the street for her. I made sure to catch up with Promise that night, and slam her hard against the side of the house.

I told her I knew what she was doing, and I said, "You may not be afraid of your grandma, but you will sure as hell be afraid of me." I was going to say more and hit her too, but the look on her face stopped me. Promise ran inside. I sat down on the steps, looked at my hands. She thought I was an enemy to her, but she didn't know it was my own mother I'd gone against.

When my mother had looked scared, there was a moment when I felt like Promise and I were winning something. I could have jumped up and down and shouted my child's name right there on the sidewalk. Even when I saw her at the house, a part of me wanted to say I loved her about a thousand times, but I didn't. I respected my mother too much.

* * *

8. World on a String

By the time she was in the eleventh grade, I wasn't using anymore, just drinking. I'd found a boyfriend, Tony, who took care of things, and we had a room in the basement for Promise. I was so excited when she came back that I even had the idea we might watch TV together like we did when she was in kindergarten, me with my arm around her, both of us eating jelly sandwiches again. But I didn't know Promise like my mother knew me, and I didn't know how to control her either.

She was gone most of the time with her special school things. I tried to ask her about them, but I never got anywhere. And one night after Tony'd knocked back three or four 40s, he thought he'd give it a try. He picked up her French book and said, "Parlez-vous français?" When she didn't answer, he started roaming around, picking up the other books and calling out their titles, acting like a little kid trying to get attention while she stood with her back to him. He picked one up and said, "*The*

Picture of Dorian Gray and Other Writings by Mr. Oscar Wilde. You know what this is, Promise? You pay attention, baby girl. This is the kind of book they read in college."

And while I said, "Is that right?" to be polite, she fished two quarters out of her pocket and gave them to me. I took them like an idiot.

"You win," Promise said. "He does know how to read." She said it like we'd made a bet. "He doesn't read well, but enough to count as literate. He even knows how to say 'college.' Who'd'a thought?"

Tony just stood there drunk and staring, and then when he said, "I can read. Who said I couldn't read?" Promise busted out laughing. Afterward, I don't think I ever did get him to believe that Promise and I weren't making fun of him behind his back, calling him ignorant and making up bets. From that day on, he stayed as far as he could from Promise. That meant I couldn't have too much to do with her either since I had to show him I was on his side.

It wasn't long before I got used to not talking to my daughter except to tell her to cover up her titties better. And when my sister came by, wanting to know where Promise was at, I tried to explain that things were different with these girls now, some of them, anyway.

When we were young, we knew better than to talk back. We respected grown people because we knew we depended on them. We even respected those men. After all, they only wanted to hold us for a while and put their thing inside. Then they paid their money. Besides, if we didn't know how to forgive and be grateful, how could we have survived?

A lot of people still understand that. My sister had four daughters, and they all knew how to act. But Promise had been born with the world on a string. She carried on like she hated us all.

* * *

9. Leaving Me

Promise's grandmother didn't come with us to the Golden Corral. She was mad because when Promise got her awards, she didn't thank her family for all we'd done for her; she only thanked her teachers. And did Promise apologize or try to make an old woman feel better? Hardly. All she did was say, "Well, Happy Graduation to me," with a big smile on her face. And no surprise that Tony didn't come either. I hardly saw him anymore, and I already knew I'd have to find a new place to live pretty soon.

Still, it had been a big group in my nephew's car. One of Promise's cousins had to sit in her sister's lap, and Promise was so happy she couldn't stop talking. Even when we were inside with our food, she wouldn't slow down, gave a whole speech about her scholarships and how she won them. My sister patted my leg and told me I'd done a good job. "You don't see any of these other knuckleheads going to college," she told me. "Promise is something else."

"She's getting a big head," I said, but I could feel my own face about to crack open, smiling. I was thinking back to when I used to walk down the street with my little baby in my arms, and it felt like the whole world was just waiting to see what we did with our lives. I didn't know I could still feel like that again. I wanted to open my mouth and crow.

"Hey, Promise," I called out, "what's it going to be? Medicine or law? Maybe you'll be a doctor *and* a lawyer."

But two of her cousins were already saying, "Journalism!" And Promise looked disgusted with me.

"Jour-no-lism, remember? That's why I'm going to Columbia. Remember? The plan since I was ten, remember?"

"But that didn't mean anything!"

The look on her face got a whole lot worse. "I guess nothing I ever said meant anything to you."

"But, Columbia's in New York," I said. "That's what you told me."

"Well good for you. You did remember one thing right." But then the ugliness went out of her face as fast as it had come in, and nothing but sadness took its place. "You should have been listening. I'm going to New York."

Sometimes I still think about how I let Promise go without even knowing what she wanted or which school she picked, and I'm pretty sure she was looking at me like that because she was sorry for both of us.

I didn't feel sorry then, though. I didn't feel anything else either. I just sat there knowing my time was up. My child was leaving me, and my insides had all turned to stone.

* * *

10. My Sister's Girls Stayed with Her

Out of the six children my sister had, she's got one son that's been killed already. The other boy is in an Idaho penitentiary with sixteen more years to go before he can even try for parole. Her daughters are all right here, though. Sometimes, all of us go out to Wilkins together. We let the girls take the better tricks, and we try to remember to write down the license plate numbers. We tell the girls to use condoms, too, and they say we nag, but they know it's because we love them. Sometimes my sister tells them they should go to college like Promise, but they never listen.

On Mother's Day, there's always a party for my sister and mother. One of them usually gets a mug or a shirt with "World's Greatest Mom" or "World's Greatest Grandma" on it. A bunch of us spend the whole morning cooking together, and it's a good day—that's what I try to think, anyway. But Promise never even sends a card, and when the call comes it's always from my nephew in prison. A lot of time, I'm out on the street by myself, too, especially in winter, while my sister sits at home with her grandkids crawling all over her. When they can, her girls try to take care of her. They don't like their mother to have to work.

* * *

11. Promise Visits

It's been eight years since Promise left for college, four years since she graduated and decided to stay in New York to work in the "media." She comes to see me every year or two, but the visits are always short and make me disappointed. I try to get her to remember the good times. Once, I said something about when she won the It's Academic Superbowl, and she got so angry at me for not going. I wish somebody had told me then that I had a child who wanted me to be with her more. I would have done things so different.

After that, I thought I needed to explain about my life and how I did the best I could. I had plenty of time, more than a year, to figure out what to say. But then I'd think about Promise and all she had going on, and it hurt too much to talk about how pitiful my own life had been. I tried another way, though. I tried to look at the good side and show Promise it all turned out for the best.

Next time she came to see me I asked her did she know why I named her Promise? She said no, and I told her it was because I made a promise to her when she was born: She wouldn't live the way I did. Her life would turn out better.

"And it came true!" I said. I remember feeling excited and even proud when I finally said it. I'd never told anyone before, and I'd been planning for months to tell it to her. I had my arms coming open like we were going to hug each other. "That's the wonderful thing, Promise. It came true."

"I'm the one who made it come true," she told me. We looked at each other again. I saw the set of her face and knew what a fool I'd been. I'd been hoping she'd say I was a good mother, or give me some credit for the way she turned out, but the truth was I didn't have any reason to hope for something like that. I only had reason to feel ashamed.

Later, right before she left, she asked why I never did anything with my life. I just told her that once you get started in a certain direction it's hard to change. She nodded.

"Shouldn't have taken that first drug," she said.

"Learn from my mistakes," I told her. She didn't need to know that I'd been ten years old the first time, or that it was her grandmother who put the needle in my helpless arm. Anyway, Promise hugged me before she left.

I went out with one of my nieces that night. It was cold, and we passed a bottle of vodka back and forth in the same weedy lot off North Washington where I'd found Promise's cell phone so many years ago. Finally, an old minivan pulled up, and she went running for it. Her Thursday night guy. He'd give her an extra twenty dollars sometimes, call her "my lady." She called him "the best man in Baltimore." Once she took off, safe with her regular, I could rest easy, get a couple Xanax out of my coat pocket, and wash them down with the last of the vodka.

Maybe an hour later, a trick pulled over for me. He looked a little disappointed when he got up close, but he still let me in. Even asked me how I was doing while he turned up the Ravens game on the radio. The guy had spots on his face, hardly any nose, kind of like a turtle.

"Feeling good," I told him. "Saw my daughter today."

Old Turtle Face turned the radio back down again. "Daughter?" he said. "You got a daughter?"

Felt something like lightning run through my body. "Yeah," I told him. "I got a daughter."

Man had the nerve to ask what she looked like.

Really? What did that sweet, sweet baby snuggling in my arms look like? Or the proudest, most beautiful girl in the world, jumping up and down because she'd just won the It's Academic Superbowl? The one who didn't know I was watching her on TV, cheering as loud as I could and crying too. The grown-up girl walking to the train station just a few hours ago, already forgetting I was even alive?

That creepy old spot-faced perv wanted to lay his eyes on her and everything else too.

"She looks like herself," I told him. "Anyway, she's gone from here."

And what I thought was: *she's gone because I always wanted her gone.* I didn't know it was possible to be so happy and so sad at the same time.

And Turtle Face? He shut up about Promise, then lit a

cigarette and gave me one. He wasn't so bad, not really. We had a smoke together before he parked in the alley.

* * *

This story first appeared in the After Dinner Conversation—May 2025 issue.

This story won Pleiades' Kinder/Crump award for short fiction and was originally published in the spring 2022 edition of Pleiades.

Discussion Questions

1. The narrator says she named her daughter Promise because she made a promise to give her a better life. Promise did, in fact, have a better life, but gives all the credit to herself. Who is right? Who deserves credit?

2. Should parents be measured by their generational improvement over the way they were parented or against some objective parenting standard?

3. Does Promise have a moral obligation to visit her mother? Should she lie to her mother about her being a good parent? What does Promise get (or lose) by cutting her mother out of her life and telling her the truth about her parenting?

4. When there is a rift between Promise and Tony, the narrator sides with Tony and spends less time with Promise. Given the narrator's living situation is this a mistake? Should a parent always side with their children against a partner? Would it matter if they were married?

5. To what extent is the narrator responsible for failing to get her life in order?

* * *

On Ice

Laura Mullen

* * *

<u>Content Disclosure</u>: None

* * *

Jacob keeps calling. The phone buzzes at inconvenient times, interrupting my morning meditation, a call with my therapist, my weekly team meeting. I silence the calls, but his name threads through my mind, interrupting my train of thought, demanding attention.

Please answer. We need to talk.

The text messages pile up as well, though I have muted notifications on his missives, protecting me from the onslaught. Dr. Novali notices my eyes darting to the screen midway through our Wednesday session, my voice catching mid-story, derailing me. She looks at the phone but doesn't ask.

"Jacob," I offer. The name is heavy with history and innuendo, and Dr. Novali raises her eyebrows.

"Have you been talking to Jacob again?"

I haven't, I assure her, and I try not to read into her tone.

Jacob has only recently stopped being the main character in my therapy sessions. I assume Dr. Novali is not eager to resurrect the topic of our failed relationship.

Before bed I scroll through dating apps on my phone, rereading long message chains I have started and abandoned with men I avoid meeting in real life. Dr. Novali says my engagement on these platforms counts as self-care, and so I swipe right and left, respond to direct messages, pretend I am interested in future moments. When Jacob calls, I am startled. Jacob's familiar face—his smile, his stubble—displaces the profile of the man I had been considering (Brandon: he likes boats and beer). I throw the phone across the bed, panicked.

"CeCe?" His voice is muffled, and I realize I have inadvertently answered the phone. I crawl from beneath the covers to retrieve it, planning to hang up, but I hear his voice. "Don't hang up."

His voice. His voice. Deep and throaty, as familiar as the voice of my mother, as distinct as any I have heard. He should record audiobooks, do voice-overs or movies or radio shows. Even two years later, his voice is intoxicating. I lift the phone to my ear, thirsty for more, but say nothing.

"CeCe, can you hear me? I don't know if you can hear me." I imagine him pulling the phone away to confirm the timer on the call is still going. I open my mouth to speak but find I cannot. "CeCe, we should talk. I think we should talk. I don't know if you got the letter from Coastal, but if you did, you need to read it. We need to make some decisions, and I have a question for you."

Still, I say nothing. I did get the letter. It was a bill, actually, accompanied by a letter. When it arrived, I set it aside, a problem for another day. It wasn't the money. Six hundred dollars wouldn't break the bank, though when I paid it each year, I wondered why I was continuing to do so, whether Jacob even knew I did. It was illogical to preserve these embryos for a future that wasn't coming.

"I got it," I say, and I hear him exhale.

"You're there. Hi. Thanks for answering."

"Hi." My voice is higher than I intend, and I realize I haven't spoken in several hours. I am surprised he receives the bills or the letters from Coastal Fertility. I wonder when he called them to update his address. The embryos are half his, I suppose, though I alone have funded them.

"How are you?"

I contemplate responses to this question. I am well. I was recently promoted at work. I am in therapy. I have morning rituals I follow with the devout rigor of a religious convert. I have my friends, my work, and my nephews nearby. I am well. If I tell him I am well he will be relieved to know he did not break me. I say nothing.

He allows a long moment to pass before he speaks. "You sound good. I'm good too. I'm back in Syracuse, you know." I do know. I ran into Mitchell—once our friend, now Jacob's friend— a year ago. Mitchell told me Jacob moved. Jacob met someone. Jacob was doing well.

"I heard."

Silence expands and I try to imagine what I will do when this call ends. How will I put it out of my mind, calm down, find sleep? What ritual will keep my mind from spinning, my thoughts from spiraling down, down, down?

"What do you want?" I ask, and I hate the harshness in my

voice. I want to be peaceful and magnanimous, not a raw open wound oozing through the phone. And yet, I sound angry. I am angry. Still.

"Did you pay the bill?"

"Not yet."

"Are you going to?"

"I don't know."

"Did you read the letter?" The letter, included in the envelope with the bill, informed me I could either pay the six-hundred-dollar annual fee to keep our seven embryos frozen, or I could opt to destroy them. The South Carolina legislature was considering a bill that would change IVF by categorizing embryos as human beings. The new law would make it a crime to destroy them. If that happens, I may be signing up to pay the six-hundred-dollar fee in perpetuity to avoid criminal charges. Or, of course, I could use them. Septo-mom.

"I'm gonna have them destroyed," I say, though I wasn't sure of it before this moment. "We aren't going to use them; I don't know why I have even saved them this long." Even as I speak, I am not sure whether I hope he will protest.

Jacob is silent and I'm surprised. I do expect him to agree, to express gratitude for making this easy, letting him off the hook, once and for all.

"I can pay it," Jacob says.

"Why?"

"I just—I may want to use them someday."

"What?"

"I mean, I may want to use them. I do want to use them."

"You want to use them? To have a baby? We haven't spoken in two years." And yet, a bubble of possibility is rising within me. I have let go of Jacob, of our life together, but with only one sentence he springs the hinge on the hope stowed deep down in my subconscious.

"No, I mean. That's not what I mean."

The surge shifts into something else—confusion? rage?—as the possibilities of his meaning trickle into my brain. "What do you mean?"

"I mean..." He pauses and I wait. "*I* want to use them. I'm seeing someone. I've been seeing someone since I moved back up here, and... it's serious. And we want kids. Someday. But, she can't—she is older. But I think we want kids. And she is open to using our embryos."

"Our embryos." Somehow, in my wildest dreams, this hasn't occurred to me. Jacob and I were together for six years before we froze the embryos. I was thirty-four, the realities of my biological clock settling over me. I wanted kids, and I wanted Jacob. I had a good, steady job and a man I loved. But he wasn't ready. The reasons, those stated and those silent, were plentiful.

Jacob worked in construction, scraping together projects, bringing on bursts of cash followed by droughts between jobs. An injury could sideline him for weeks, and years of playing rugby had left him with a bad back. He needed to find something steady, a job with benefits. He needed to be worthy of me, of our potential children. He needed a cortisone shot, one big job, a new certification—and, it turned out, a different woman. Still, back then I heard *reasons* rather than excuses, and I pushed him to make the embryos. To preserve the option.

"Hopefully we won't ever need them," I had said. "When we are ready, hopefully, I'll just get pregnant naturally. This is just a precaution, so we have the option." I had watched my friends struggle through miscarriages and IVF, through cycles of hope and loss and pain. He listened to me describe it, of course, but his knowledge wasn't intimate. Still, he agreed, and we went through the process, the hormone injections, the extraction, the insemination, and genetic testing. In the end, we got seven—a great yield—and I relaxed. The future could take its time.

"No," I say now. "You can't use them."

I try to conjure the woman Jacob is *seeing*. The woman he is ready to have children with. The woman he gets out of bed for each day. By the time we ended, Jacob hadn't gotten out of bed or left the house in months. He wouldn't see a therapist, wouldn't go to physical therapy, or take medication. He was in quicksand, slipping beneath the grains with a resignation that seemed intentional. He would rather sink to the depths of the hole than rise to the heights of my expectations.

Jacob had always struggled with depression. Years of therapy have helped me to see the darkness was a part of what made him attractive. My urge to save him, my satisfaction in being the light in someone's life. I liked to be his one good thing. It was a role that made sense to me. Until it didn't.

Dr. Novali would say I was repeating a pattern. I had seen my father make sacrifices to support my mother through her battle with cancer—a valiant, eight-year struggle that ended in defeat. And then it was me who learned to swallow my desires in the interest of the family. I needed to be home after school for Evan and Jade. I needed to stay close to home rather than flee far for college. My value was equal to my contributions. It never occurred to me that it should be different.

It didn't start that way with Jacob. When we met, I was

working in publishing, eager to climb the ladder, thrilled to work in the literary world with so many others whose lives had also been shaped more by characters and plots than actual human interaction. When we met, he was happy and hopeful, planning a home remodeling business that would give him financial and creative freedom. We could see our futures unfolding, side-by-side, a gorgeous pursuit of our separate dreams. Jacob didn't have a bad day for the first year we were together, and when the first one arrived, my response was a reflex. A work trip canceled, a conference missed, emails delayed. It felt good to take care of him. It felt good to be needed, for a while.

Eventually, his needs grew heavy. I was not a young girl trapped in my childhood home. I had glimpsed another version of life, experienced joy derived from dreams and talent. His bad days were repeated, sometimes growing into weeks and months, a crushing heaviness I bore with silent fury, tallying the friendships, the plans, the future we were losing. Still, I said nothing. I longed for change; I was terrified of losing him.

Jacob is talking again. "I know it's a big deal, and it's probably a surprise, and—we can talk. We should talk. I want you to meet Adrienne. You'll like her. And we can work out whatever you want; we can work it out."

"No."

"CeCe, please consider it. Please think about it."

"No. No. Those are mine. You can't use them."

"But you've been paying to keep them frozen. Were you thinking you would use them someday?"

"I don't know. Maybe. I didn't think about it."

"Well. But. I mean. You did keep them." He says it as

though this is evidence to support some theory. The truth rises in me and I swallow it. I don't say: *I kept them for us.* I don't tell him I am keeping them frozen to keep the ember alive. It is too sad. Too pathetic.

"So you're ready to have kids now?" I hear the bite in my tone, and it sounds petty. Resentful.

"Yeah. I'm sorry, CeCe. I'm sorry."

I hang up the phone, simmering with the indignity of the conversation, of the entire situation. Jacob is doing *well*. I had imagined him across town, living in a dim basement apartment, eating ramen and Cheetos and cans of peas, playing *Call of Duty* late into the night. I had pictured him gaining weight, losing money, feeling miserable. Sometimes I had imagined his funeral, myself—grieving—embraced by his family and friends. I pictured him realizing, one day, what he had lost, and coming to claim it. Even when Mitchell told me Jacob moved and met someone, I resisted the reality.

Now I imagine Adrienne. How old could she be? I am thirty-eight. Jacob is forty. Adrienne wants to implant my young egg into her body. How old is she? I picture crow's-feet and gray roots, his strong hands massaging her slackening skin. *No.* I haul myself out of bed and down the stairs, unearthing the Coastal letter and the bill.

Did you think of using them? I haven't. But I have taken comfort in their existence. Their existence allows me to turn down dates, to brand the last two years as "rebuilding years" for focusing on myself. *It's the year of Cecelia*, I say each January, as though I am in charge of my life. As though I am alone by choice.

I lift the Coastal Fertility envelope from the mail tray on

the marble countertop and reread the letter, considering my options. Seven embryos. If it were an even number, perhaps we could split them, each able to do what we wish. A friend once pointed out all seven of our embryos are technically twins, conceived at the same time. We could birth a basketball team of siblings, raised in different states, different homes. It would be a scientific study of nature versus nurture. Would they be depressives and martyrs like Jacob and I? Or could we nurture that out of them?

I could use them myself—have the baby Jacob and I had intended, raise him or her on my own. It wouldn't be a betrayal of Jacob. I wouldn't do it with another man, implant the embryo into someone else's body, pretend a third person plays some part in the biology of our creation. I would do it alone. Would it bring Jacob back to me—a creature made from our two halves, a baby sleeping in the sunlit second-floor back bedroom we always said would be a nursery?

I put the letter down again and wedge my feet into the sneakers near the front door. It is late but I need to move, to sweat the conversation with Jacob out of my mind. My phone dings while I am running, my heart racing, perspiration pouring down my face and chest. I ignore it, not ready to see any more from Jacob.

When I slow to a walk near my house, I look at my phone and see the notification was not from Jacob after all. It was Matt R., from my dating app. Matt R. wants to meet. Matt R. thinks we have a lot in common.

"Sure Matt," I type, though Matt and I surely do not have anything in common. "Let's have coffee tomorrow."

"How about I make you dinner at my place?"

The exchange—the push and pull of plans and power—is already exhausting. How do people do this? "How about coffee?" I reiterate, and he relents. I hope he drinks coffee. In our last year together, Jacob renounced caffeine, blaming it for the rise and fall of his psyche. Coffee became my guilty pleasure, sipped furtively at work, scrubbed from my breath before I walked in the door.

"Coffee sounds good. See you tomorrow."

I shower and then crawl back into bed to indulge in my worst habit: getting drunk on nostalgia. On my phone, I scroll through pictures of Jacob and me from years ago, searching for signs of what would come. But, as usual, there are no signs. There are no photos of the piles of laundry, the unwashed dishes, the disappointment I felt when I walked in the door at the end of each and every day, month after month. The pictures are bright, a portrait of a happy couple.

Why her? I text Jacob before I can help myself. It is embarrassing to ask and yet, it is all I can think of. Who is this Adrienne? What about her lets him rise each day with hope for the future?

He doesn't reply, and I think this is a gift. Or maybe he's just gone to sleep.

* * *

When I meet Matt for coffee the next morning, I am pleasantly surprised to find he is a clean-shaven freelance journalist who was previously married to his college girlfriend. (I have found divorcees are better than bachelors, at my age.) He orders a black coffee and swallows it like medicine. Like me, he has been on the apps for three years, and like me, he appears bored by the predictability of each question and each answer.

"Do you want kids?" he asks as though he already knows my response.

I nod, because I have always wanted kids. It isn't a hard question. It's just become hard to say it out loud, as the years have passed, the possibility dimming.

Matt says he wants kids *someday*, a familiar code indicating he is no different than the hundred dates that preceded him. Nonetheless, his sense of humor is self-deprecating and disarming, he pauses to consider before answering my questions and leans in to listen intently when I speak. He tells me he started cycling as a way to release tension, a recommendation from his therapist, and I am intrigued by this man who is curious and confident enough to seek help. We plan to meet for dinner the following weekend, giving each of us four days to formulate a plausible reason to cancel.

It is two days later when Jacob's reply to my question arrives. *I don't know.* And although I am in the middle of a meeting with my team, I read it and then go off camera, surprised by the tears that fall. I don't know what I wanted him to say. I don't know what words would be a salve.

Later that evening, alone in my house, I see I have a new email from Coastal Fertility.

Please complete the attached form to indicate your consent to destroy Embryos #74832, #27483, #37281...

I read it several times. I have not yet asked for the embryos to be destroyed. This must be Jacob's doing, and it feels like an act of love. One last kindness, a concession to my wishes. How do they destroy embryos? I imagine them thawing, softening, becoming vulnerable. I close the email, not sure whether I am ready to give up on the potential those blobs of

DNA represent.

I think of Matt's question, of the clarity I felt when I nodded my head. I want kids. I am just afraid it won't happen for me. Wanting has become a dangerous, vulnerable thing.

In the morning, I call Coastal Fertility and wait on hold for a surprisingly long time before a woman answers, her voice strained. She introduces herself as Susan and apologizes for the wait. "Obviously we are experiencing a much higher than usual call volume." I imagine the other women calling in—the women desperate for babies, the women who froze embryos before going through chemo, the women who had tried everything else before emptying their savings for Coastal Fertility—somehow, I never thought of them before.

"I wanted to know whether it was possible to preserve some of my embryos but not all of them," I say, and Susan explains the change it will cause in my billing, the method they use to select which to preserve, the timing for destruction. It echoes the roadmap that guided my past experience: a literal application of *survival of the fittest*. Four years earlier nineteen eggs were harvested from my thirty-four-year-old uterus, thirteen of which survived insemination. After genetic testing, only seven remained viable, deemed optimal specimens. The others were destroyed, though it hadn't felt like murder.

"My ex requested that all seven embryos be destroyed. If I consent, but decide to retain one or two, will he be notified that some have been retained?"

"He will be notified if you attempt to use the embryos while they are in our care because his name is on the account, but honestly, if I were you, I would transfer whichever ones you want to keep out of the state. I don't know how long we will be able to stay open with the way the laws are changing. The doctors are worried about their own liability."

"How would that work?"

She explains the intricacies of exporting the embryos and it is clear she has given the speech many times.

I tell her I will think it over and hang up, letting the possibilities settle over me. I look again at the email requesting my consent. I imagine Jacob's conversation with Adrienne, the way he settles into his chair before delivering bad news, looking down while he speaks and then looking up, into my—her—eyes to gauge the reaction. Had Adrienne really wanted this—to carry his ex-girlfriend's baby in her body? We'd never even met. What did she know of me—who was I in the story Jacob told? Maybe a part of her would be relieved to take this option off the table. Maybe not. Would she show her dismay? My disappointment used to deflate him, so I hid my desires, my successes, my expectations. I buried myself in the hope of resurrecting him.

When Jacob left, I was bereft. For two years, I have inventoried the opportunities I missed, the ways I went wrong, the love I let slip through my fingers. I've relived the day he left—the day he rallied himself to pack bags, to say goodbye—countless times, imagining the fierce pressure of his arms around me, the hug I didn't believe would be our last. I had waited and begged and promised I would change. I had committed to demanding less, accepting his depression, his limitations. But still he left.

I imagine Adrienne—whoever she is—now bearing the burden of Jacob's emotions. I feel a heaviness that may be jealousy or may be something else. Empathy? Maybe. For a moment I am Adrienne, sitting on a sofa in a room far north of here, the sky outside eternally gray. I hold my breath as I consider my response, measure my reaction before revealing it, a habit too entrenched to erase. I see myself cross the room to Jacob, sit on his lap, collapse into the hard warmth of him, luxuriate in his embrace. I feel his release, relief. But when the Adrienne version of me stands, she is heavy with all that went unsaid. She must wonder whether he will be happy without children. Wonder how he can love her and also want children who are half of me. She must yearn for him to see the feelings she cannot voice.

I look at the phone in front of me. I could call Jacob and talk it through. I could explain my reservations, my fears, my need to keep a sliver of hope alive for the future I once thought I owned. He would listen and sigh deeply, unable to make a decision, unable to give me what I want. He will not surprise me. I don't call him.

With a blue pen, I mark up the consent form before I sign it, modifying it to reflect my own preferences—the only ones that matter anymore. I use my phone to scan and email it back to Coastal Fertility. I find I am relieved. Almost grateful for the unilateral decision. I don't have to live in reaction to him anymore. I don't have to accept his open arms, his broad chest—his good intentions—as consolation for his shortcomings. I can make a choice without apology or explanation. This is the silver lining to my loss: when Jacob left, he released me. He gifted me a freedom I have refused to see, my back to the door for all this time.

I hesitate before I text Jacob, indulging in a fantasy of defiance. If I didn't text him, would he ever ask? Probably not. But I reach out anyway, another pesky habit, the need for a period at the end of a paragraph.

All done. I write. Because what's done is done.

* * *

I am reviewing a presentation for work when my personal email dings. Coastal Fertility has sent me an extraction form for the two remaining embryos. I open the PDF and fill it out. Both embryos will be transferred to a clinic in Pennsylvania. When I sign, I release the clinic from liability in the event the embryos are damaged during their transition. Susan assured me the embryos would remain in a deep freeze through the transfer, unscathed by the shifting landscape, but now I contemplate car crashes and broken cooling systems.

I have a date with Matt the next evening. We meet for dinner and stay for dessert, ordering decaf cappuccinos to extend our time together. We talk about our jobs, our families of origin, our hobbies—he wants me to try cycling with him, and it occurs to me that relationships can open doors, push you out of your comfort zone. I confess that bikes hurt my butt.

"But you'll get used to it after a few times. You have to keep riding through that pain."

"I'll get used to the pain? Or it will stop hurting?"

He laughs like I'm joking. "It stops hurting. You just can't give up after the first time or you won't get to the other side of it."

Conversation turns to the week ahead and the week we just finished. Fueled by the bottle of wine we drank, or maybe just the sense of intimacy we have created at our candlelit corner table, I tell him about the embryos, the need to move them out of the state. I focus on the absurdity of the situation to avoid the pinch of pain the topic raises in me.

"Can you imagine wanting to use the embryos in some other woman? I mean, she has never even met me."

Matt nods thoughtfully, considering. Perhaps he, like me, is trying to picture this woman. "Did you say yes?"

"No. I said no."

"Are you planning to use them?"

"I don't know. Not right now." I want to tell him that I destroyed some—but only some—of them, that I kept two as a nest egg for myself, an insurance policy. But I don't go into the details.

"It's kind of lovely," he observes, and I wonder where he is going with this. "The potential they represent. The possibility. If one of you were to pass away, you could leave a legacy with those embryos."

I wonder if I can be with a man who says *pass away* instead of *die*. His impulse to sugarcoat is suddenly repulsive. I wish I hadn't told him about the embryos. I moved too fast. The only thing less sexy than the harsh realities of fertility planning is a man's opinion on the topic.

"Well, hopefully, no one dies any time soon." I look for the waiter, suddenly desperate to leave. I picture my embryos preparing for their trip, moving north into a new climate, resilient when confronted with transition.

* * *

Three days later Matt texts me a news article about a South Carolina fertility clinic torched by political protestors. *Good thing you're getting your little guys out of dodge,* he writes.

I click through the link, annoyed by his use of the phrase *little guys* to describe a pile of cells. The picture that comes up on the screen is familiar, and my breath catches. It is not *some* fertility clinic. It is Coastal Fertility, still standing, though the windows are blown out, the insides clearly charred.

I freeze, holding my breath as I scroll through the article. No one was harmed. The fire was set in the middle of the night, and the culprit has already been identified: Marjorie Maynor, the leader of a local True Patriots group who was a loud voice on the issue of fetal personhood. She is in custody, apparently unavailable for a quote. The paper dug up old talking points from her Facebook page where she decried IVF as legalized murder and wrote lengthy rants about God's intentions. The article includes a link to her personal page and the page of True Patriots.

Matt sends a follow-up article in which a representative for the True Patriots praises Marjorie Maynor's vigilante approach to justice and appears surprised that the facility not only conducted fertility treatments but also housed embryos. *I hope yours are all right,* Matt texts.

I want to send the article to Jacob, but Jacob thinks the embryos were already destroyed. I consider replying to Matt but don't want to try to explain the sharp wound opening inside of me as I review images of the scorched facility. I call Coastal, hoping to talk with Susan, but get a busy tone. I wonder whether my last two embryos were extracted before the match was struck. Maybe they are safe in Pennsylvania.

I've avoided imagining the possibilities the two remaining embryos represent. Their preservation somehow made it possible for me to let go of the future I had attached to the seven test tubes Jacob and I had created.

I dial the clinic again and am again met with only a flat beep, droning into my ear. I won't have answers today. I may not tomorrow. I rest my phone on the counter and turn on the television. On the local news, Marjorie Maynor's face looks haggard. I try to direct my anger in her direction, the villain in this tale. But I can't rouse myself to hate her. I feel something else, something dull and empty I can't quite name.

I turn the television off and go out the back door to the shed, where my bike rests against a wall, tires deflated, a layer of grimy dust covering the bright red bars I once admired. I touch the seat tentatively, its firm confidence a threat, and wheel it into the sunlight, using my sleeve to remove some of the black crust from the frame. There is a pump in the shed, and I fill the tires, using more strength than I expected. The exertion is soothing.

I bought this bike three years earlier, an initiative to get Jacob out of the house, to give us a shared hobby. He had mounted his with a grimace and made it a few blocks before stopping and walking it home. I apologized, seeing my miscalculation, and walked home beside him. It was hot that day, the sun punishing, and I longed to climb onto my new bike and feel the wind in my hair, to soar over routes that took ages to walk. But it felt like bragging, my ability to fly.

I mount the bike unsteadily, pedaling down my driveway and out to the street. I want to stay on the sidewalk, protected from passing cars and the tyranny of traffic laws, but I veer into the street instead, living dangerously. My neighborhood breezes by, familiar facades a flash in the passing scenery.

When I get to Coastal Fertility, I am drenched in sweat, the humidity oppressive and draining. I let my bike fall to the ground and sit on the curb to survey the scene in front of me. There is yellow tape around the building, one car still in the parking lot, trapped by the ongoing investigation. I run my fingers over the spikes of grass lining the curb, appreciating their tough resilience, their consistency. My finger catches on a stem, softer and juicier than its neighboring growth, and I close my fingers around it, snapping it, lifting the yellow dandelion head to my nose. I recall vaguely that a yellow flower can reveal a love of butter or evolve into a puff you blow on to make a wish.

Before I mount my bike, I cross the street to rest the flower on the curb in front of the burned-out building, gently exhaling the last of my wishes for this place. The ride home feels longer than the ride there, and I know when I wake in the morning I will ache.

I snap a picture of my bike and text it to Matt. *Got her out of retirement this morning.*

His response is almost immediate. *Nice! If you aren't too sore tomorrow, let me show you my favorite trail.*

I go back outside and look at the bike, still dirty. When I touch the seat, the handlebars, I imagine the bike is humming its gratitude in my direction, preening, hoping to be touched and used.

"What do you think?" I ask it out loud. "Should we ride again?"

* * *

It is nearly a month before someone answers the phone at Coastal Fertility, a young man who I picture wearing a suit in a skyscraper, the undertaker for the facility's carcass. I read out all seven embryo numbers from the letter I had received, bracing to learn their fate.

"Yeah, I have the records. It looks like the three slated for destruction were lost in the fire, but the four selected for relocation had already been removed. They should be safely in New York by now."

It takes me a moment to understand what he is saying. Four? New York? "You mean Pennsylvania. Two in Pennsylvania."

"Oh yes. I'm sorry. Two in Pennsylvania"—I release the breath I had held. That makes more sense. He continues—"and two in Syracuse, New York."

"I'm sorry. I only requested the transfer of two embryos. To Pennsylvania. Who requested the other two?" Though of course, I know. The voice on the phone confirms that Jacob filed the request for removal the day after I did. I look back through our messages. He must have done it when he received my text message.

All done, I had written.

And he thought I was.

* * *

This story first appeared in the After Dinner Conversation—January 2025 issue.

Discussion Questions

1. What are the factors that cause a person to "move on" after a breakup? Why is Cecelia having so much trouble moving on?

2. What individual rights should Cecelia and Jacob have to the fertilized eggs being retained? Would you support a law enshrining those rights, or should they be rights based on the conversation between the two parties?

3. Cecelia has been going to therapy for two years related to her breakup with Jacob. Is the fact that she is still struggling with their breakup proof the therapy isn't working? How do you know if therapy is working?

4. If either Cecelia or Jacob used one of the fertilized eggs with a new partner to make a baby, do they have an obligation to tell the other? Would you rather know, or not know, you have your biological child out in the world? Why or why not?

5. If Jacob was the one struggling with depression and other issues, why is he the one that ended the relationship? What (*if anything*) does that tell you about each of them and their relationship?

* * *

J u n k

Taylor Lawritson

* * *

<u>Content Disclosure</u>: Terminal Illness; Depiction of Alcohol Use; Trauma and PTSD; Strong Language

* * *

At first it was just bottle caps. And you might laugh at that. You might think 'what kind of sentimentality is there in a bottle cap?' But that's a dumb question because what type of sentimentality is there to anything?

We control the sentimentality.

You control the sentimentality.

I control the sentimentality.

Heather told me that affirmations work. You can apparently retrain your brain on them if you really believe them. So I have to tell myself that I control the objects and the objects don't control me. And I have to believe it. The affirmations have to be about me and not about the objects. She says that sentimentality isn't really real, I mean you can't actually touch it. Objects only have their function and if the function is only sentimentality then actually they have no function because sentiment is a made-up thing in your brain. I like Heather because she makes sense. What use is the necklace that you're wearing? Maybe it reminds you of your sixteenth birthday or your first boyfriend. And that's silly. Really. Look at yourself. That necklace is more of a choking hazard than anything, isn't it? If somebody really needed to get you out of the picture they could just grab that bad boy and pull until your lights go dark. But you keep it because it's like you can almost feel that first boyfriend's fingers on the clasp, getting the baby hairs on your neck stuck in the chain. You remember how you turned around and felt sure that this tiny chain was going to wrap around the life you imagined and choke you both together forever. You keep the necklace because you want to remember that certainty. But really you can remember it on your own. You don't need the necklace. It's all in your head. You just don't trust yourself.

Heather says it helps to just think about them as objects. Not to give them a name or a shape. Just leave them as lumps in your brain. Objects. It's a little sterile, but it works to the point. They're just objects. Your necklace. My bottle caps. They're the same now. "You have to retrace the object attachment." Heather says this as she sits behind her desk, always a pen tapping at her chin. We are engaged in a dance routine and she is keeping time.

"But I want it. I need it." I stumble.

"What do you need it for?" She glides right behind.

"It's sentimental." We go around and around.

For one whole hour every Wednesday, Heather reminds me, not in so many words, that objects are evil little things. They're self-serving organisms that simply do not want to be thrown away. You can picture it the way I do if you want: objects having imaginary barbs on long, skinny arms that plant themselves into your brain so that when you try to dispose of them they yank and yank and drag themselves through your memories and out your tear ducts so before you know it you're clutching that necklace to your chest and remembering senior prom and cursing yourself for thinking you could ever live without that ugly little pendant.

It's like with the bottle caps. That's what Heather and I are working on right now.

"Start small." That's what Heather says when I get overwhelmed. But it's almost like the bottle caps are the biggest part of it. They're the whole foundation for all the other junk that's piled up through the years, like the world's ugliest pyramid. And maybe you're still skeptical about the bottle caps. But honestly, think about how stupid your high school boyfriend was. You might still wonder how a bottle cap gets sentimental the way a cheesy necklace does. But, maybe some of us never got necklaces. Maybe the only thing we ever had was bottle caps.

For a long time my dad was my only friend. My only ally. Up until I was in middle school, every night when I said my prayers and imagined talking to god, it was dad's face I was looking into. And sure, every kid worships their parents a little bit. But maybe not everybody feels like they're growing up seeking forgiveness. I had killed my mother the day I was born. And they had a choice too. Both of them, because she asked him, too. She said, "Joe, I want this baby to live." I know he regretted it, but he never said that and that's a very compassionate thing to do. Imagine the heavy burden that is. You go to the hospital, where the love of your life dies, and then you get stuck with a baby and nobody to help you raise it. So I never blamed him for the drinking. I knew it was bad. I heard the other kids' parents talking in Sunday school. But I wasn't going to fault him for rubbing Novocain on a stab wound. The drinking really barely affected me. He still woke me up for school in the morning, dunked my head in the kitchen sink, and brushed my hair back into a rubber band before sending me off. If anything, the drinking made me feel closer to him. We both paid our flaws no mind. I was a born killer and he was a drunk.

I loved him. And that's why I love those bottle caps. Loved. Loved them. Not anymore. I do not love them anymore. I don't. Really.

I *loved* them because my drunk of a father used to gather up a handful of them as soon as the big yellow school bus dropped me at the mailbox. I'd drop my backpack in a dusty patch of front lawn and run forward with my hands cupped together outstretched as if they wanted to get to the bounty before my father noticed who they belonged to. "How'd we do today, partner?" I'd say kneeling down at the lawn chair throne.

"Well, partner, I reckon we done ourselves pretty good," he'd drawl. Sometimes he would slur, but only when my memory is not feeling generous. Because he just talked slow, my dad, he just used long vowels and that was just how he talked and I am trying to become a more generous person.

Dad gave them to me because he thought I'd be able to sell them for candy money. He'd worked at the aluminum casting facility up in Hastings a long time ago and he always promised that one day he'd drive me up there to cash in my bottle cap treasure for thirty-five cents a pound. We never got around to it. The drive was two and a half hours one way and the bottle caps probably wouldn't have even covered the cost of gas in dad's pickup. But it didn't matter much to me. Those bottle caps were the currency of my father's affection.

When it was warm out, dad and I would walk to Sticky's liquor store hand in hand, Johnny Cash spilling out of the beat-up Walkman on his hip. We'd walk down the aisles and squint real hard, locked in thorough analysis of the familiar selection.

"I bet you this IPA isn't even from India." I'd posture, gingerly holding out a bottle with an idyllic mountain scene on the label.

"Well, at least we've got Ol' Reliable," he'd say, lifting a twenty-four-pack of Coors Banquets from a shelf.

"Bankies have the best caps anyways."

At home, dad would grab two Banquet chicken pot pies out of the freezer and drain a beer, while I put *For the Roses* on the record player. As Joni Mitchell echoed through the kitchen, bouncing off the hollow linoleum floors, dad would fill his first empty with pop for me and grab a second for himself. He'd shove the pies into the microwave and we'd hoist ourselves up onto either side of the sink, just in time to clink our bottles and sing along to the album opener.

> *Some get the gravy*
> *And some get the gristle*
> *Some get the marrow bone*
> *And some get nothing*
> *Though there's plenty to spare*

I always thought dad had a great voice. It's funny the things you forget. Now when I picture him, bottle neck to his lips like a microphone, I can't even remember what he sounded like. In all of my memories, Joni Mitchell's voice spills out of my father's mouth as if he were a ventriloquist's dummy. There's no proper way to mourn I guess, but looking back on the months after his death, I wish I had snapped that record in half, instead of playing it over and over. Sometimes, I watch those months back as if from behind a two-way mirror, banging on the glass, begging myself to stop listening before I drown him out forever. But the panic just makes it worse. It's like reaching down to pet the dog that was just sitting at your feet only to realize there's nothing there. At first you simply reach a little further, maybe your spatial reasoning was off. But then you have to look down and visually confront the absence. You start to get that sinking feeling that something's missing, and as you check each room in the house you feel the emptiness begin to eat up more space. You go outside, you ask around the neighborhood, you spend hours making Lost Dog posters on the library Xerox machine. You try to submerge yourself in the act of looking so that you don't have to face the inevitable act of losing. And as the loss creeps closer, you become desperate. You drive up and down the road, you call the pound, you tear the house apart.

But the emptiness comes. It always does. The first time I forgot my father's voice, I was remembering him singing "Banquet" in the kitchen. And even after he had stopped singing, Joni Mitchell stayed. The microwave beeped. He placed the pot pies on the table. We sat down and bowed our heads for a moment. Then he looked up at me, grinning above his Banquet pot pie, and extended his Banquet bottle toward mine. Joni Mitchell used his mouth to say, "Back in the banquet line!"

I spent weeks trying to get him back. I combed through

every memory I had of him hunting for just a word, a phrase. I laid on the threadbare carpet in our living room for hours in silence, waiting for the sound to come back to me. After the second day, I even found a video on YouTube called "Reconnect with Passed Loved Ones in Spirit: Guided Meditation" and I played it on a loop waiting for it to hypnotize me into remembering again. After a week, I couldn't remember anyone's voice, even my own. Whenever somebody came to the front desk at the library to ask me a question, I stared blankly ahead. I started getting lost on my way home from work.

After two weeks Mr. Harrison, the short, blueberry-shaped man who runs the library, asked me if I wanted time off. Actually, he really didn't ask. He bumbled up to the circulation desk, patting his mustache anxiously, making sure it was still there.

"I, uh well, we, uh. Well, hello."

I did not look up from the computer. He cleared his throat to fill the silence before continuing on.

"Well, yes, uh, hmmm. So! I've been thinking, you know, you've been through so much this past year. And you've come in every day and you're really a great librarian! Simply could not run the place without you! Nosirree! That's for sure!" He chuckled joylessly and fiddled with the buttons we kept in a plate next to the computer like he didn't have one pinned to his lapel at that very moment. They were small black pins with white block letters over a cartoon drawing of the solar system that said 'Reading is out of this world!!!'

"Ah yes! These are really very clever. Always give me a good chuckle. Really some of your best work I must say. Anyways, well, yes. I've decided you could use some time off.

You take such good care of the library, but maybe you should have some time to take care of yourself? Right? Yes. Yes. Take all the time you need. We'll be waiting when you're good and ready. And if you need a thing please do not hesitate to call." I stared blankly at him. He extended a hand as if to pat me on the back but seemed to think better of it, pulling it back at the last second and cradling it with the other arm like I had bitten him.

I don't remember how long I spent at home, but I do remember days bleeding together until I couldn't conceive of anything outside of the house's clapboard walls. I was wandering around the house trying to remember what each room was for, when I stumbled upon the door to the garage and became convinced that I had never seen it before. I yanked it open and stooped into the inky blackness before me, forgetting there was a step and landing face down on what felt like a trash bag full of rocks. Liquid began to trickle into my mouth and as I scrambled onto all fours to cover my bloodied nose, something sharp became implanted in my knee. My hands seemed to move of their own volition and gripped the offending object tightly, like a punishment.

I gasped as I realized that whatever it was, it would not be crushed without a fight. In an act of revenge, it had created a deep hexagonal imprint in my palm which I could already feel becoming red and angry. Suddenly exhausted, I retreated back into the house, sliding on my butt back over the threshold and laying in the mouth of the doorway. I laid there for a long time before I realized I was still clutching something in my left hand. My fingers unfurled shakily, revealing a red Coors bottle cap nestled innocently in my flushed palm. It felt impossibly warm and I wondered if it had leached away all of my body heat. I ran my fingers over its ridged side, turning it over for I don't know how long, before an image just like this one rose up inside of my head like some kind of dual reality.

There was the Coors cap on my palm, just like it was right now, but my hand was so small and the colors were different. The bottle cap in my hand was a dark, angry red. This other cap seemed almost orange. Sunlight! It was sunlight! Suddenly I looked up, but I didn't at all. I kept sitting and staring at the bottle cap in my hand. And there he was.

"Well, partner, I reckon we done ourselves pretty good."

I cried a lot. The screaming kind. I beat my hands and fists on the living room floor and I made noise for the first time in who knows how long. I yelled so loud I bet he heard me wherever he is, but I hope he didn't because I didn't mean to call him a drunk son of a bitch.

Afterwards, when I had cried myself dry and screamed myself hoarse, I stood up to change my shirt, which had become crusted with nose blood. The walls began to spin and I realized I couldn't remember the last thing I ate. I hobbled over to the freezer and pulled out six Banquet chicken pot pies. I put them all in the oven together for an hour. Then I smoothed down each of the boxes and placed them at the kitchen table like place mats.

The chicken pot pies were still frozen in the middle. The crusts were burned and crispy but inside the chicken and gravy remained congealed and frosty. I ate them anyway. All six. Every last disgusting partially frozen bite. I washed the tins and put them in a cupboard. I dragged the trash bags of bottle caps from the garage into the living room and laid on top of them like a bean bag chair. Whenever I stirred, they clinked together in response.

I'd moved the bottle caps into the garage when dad got too sick to keep walking back to his bedroom at the back of the house. When he moved into my room, which was much closer to the kitchen and the living room, I'd gutted the closet to make room for the oxygen tanks, meaning that the bottle cap collection had to be relocated. I'd done my best to forget about the months my father spent dying on our couch, but finally there on my sea of bottle caps, I surrendered. I let the pain and the guilt and the anger wash over me.

He got sick right before my college graduation. The deal was that he'd let me come home if I tried to finish my last semester. So I did. I emailed all of my professors and went back to campus a handful of times to turn things in and move my stuff. When I was gone I had to make sure somebody would watch over him, but we didn't really have friends or family in McCook. So I went to the yellow pages and called a babysitting service to come watch him. I went back to work at the library so I could finally get him a nice TV. He still preferred his record player though. Everyday I'd go to the handful of thrift stores in the area looking for new records. Carly Simon. Creedence Clearwater Revival. Three Dog Night. I bought him books too. Baldwin. Nabokov. Updike. Paperbacks, hardbacks, graphic novels, magazines, cookbooks. He didn't like to read but I figured it'd be best if he had them in case he wanted them. I bought him all kinds of things. Stuffed animals, inflatable palm trees, a little kiddie pool to soak his feet in, novelty wall signs to make him laugh and brighten the place up. He didn't really care for most of it, and he started getting really angry the last few months, and then just tired, but sometimes he'd smile and so I kept hunting for things that would make him forget for a second.

He smoked like a chimney those last few months. I didn't stop him. He got skinnier and skinnier and pretty soon he wouldn't even eat Banquet pot pies. The sores kept crawling up his legs, until they were black to the knee, and kept going. In the last month or two he barely moved from the couch. He was only awake a few hours a day, during coughing fits. Then he'd ask for a cigarette and fall back asleep.

He refused to let me hire a nurse or take him to a hospice. "The best you can do for me kiddo is find me some pot." So I did.

I loaded a bowl and held it up to his mouth. He sputtered the smoke out in a fit of wet coughs, but he grinned like a madman all the same.

"I'm probably not gonna win the dad of the year award this time, am I? Should I try for next year?"

"You're a shoo-in."

I put on *For the Roses* and hoped he'd sing along, even though I knew that he couldn't. When I sat down after flipping the record, I watched a tear drop from his nose.

"This might be the first time I haven't believed that Joni Mitchell would make everything better."

He was cold on the couch a few days later. He looked more peaceful than I'd seen him in a long time. His funeral was small, but a few of the guys from the railyard came, and some of my friends from high school, and Sticky of Sticky's liquor and the stern grandma from the babysitting agency. My diploma came in the mail about a week after he died. It's in the garage filing cabinet next to all the funeral brochures. I made five hundred in case we needed extra.

After he died, I didn't know what to do so I simply carried on as if everything was the same. I kept buying records and books and stuffed animals and anything I could find. And I kept all the things he touched. Because after he died it was so quiet. And I wanted to pretend he was still there. So I kept the lawn chair on the lawn, and I started buying new ones, wherever I could find them, until our front yard looked like a graveyard barbecue. I moved all the bottle caps back into the room he had stayed in. I bought a white noise machine because I'd gotten so used to the sound of his oxygen tank.

I never wanted to throw any of it away. Not once. Even though it'd take me a half an hour to walk through the house. Even though I eventually had to start sleeping on top of all the "Get Well Soon" stuffed animals I bought him. Even though there were too many records to even set the record player down on a flat surface and too many inflatable palm trees to watch the TV. Even after a pile of books fell on me once and I was stuck there half the night and an hour late to work.

About a year or two after dad died, I went to the laundromat. Our washer and dryer had stopped working but I couldn't bear to part with them, not with all the duct tape handiwork dad had put in to keep those things running. So I started going to the laundromat, Sunday mornings to wash my clothes and sheets and towels and things. I'm much cleaner than whatever people want you to expect from a person like me.

Anyways, I was sitting in front of the laundromat in my dad's beat-up old truck, listening to "Cold Blue Steel and Sweet Fire," when somebody knocked on my window. After nearly shitting myself, I rolled my window down, and there's this guy.

"This is a great song."

"Yeah."

"Mind if I listen with you?" I should have said no. Really because what a perfect way to get murdered. But it was 9 AM on a Sunday and I had a knife so I figured why not. And I was lonely. Heather thinks it's important I say that when it's true. So I was lonely. So he climbed into the passenger seat and I realized I didn't really know what to say.

"Nasty habit." He pointed at my cigarette.

"I mean I've practically quit. This is the last one." I was preparing to light another.

"Well, if that's the last one, I guess this one's for me." He reached over and grabbed the new cigarette out of my hand and lit it with his own lighter. I wanted to spit on him but for some reason I laughed. He reached over to turn the volume on the radio up.

"Man this is a really killer flute solo." He'd started humming at this point.

"Did you know it's the same guy on flute, saxophone, clarinet, and triangle? He plays four different instruments on this one song." I don't know why I said anything. I didn't mean to.

After the song ended, we walked into the laundromat together and he loaned me quarters as payback for the cigarette. I didn't realize how long we'd been talking until my dryer was buzzing and he was asking what I did with my time.

"I, uh, I go to Goodwill, I guess, the dollar store, Walmart sometimes. I don't really know. I listen to records maybe."

And so for a whole year, Jared courted me on my porch. We'd go browsing and then he'd drive me back home and sit on my porch while I grabbed the record player. Once he turned all the old lawn chairs around so they were facing us, like we were giving a concert. I told him about my dad. About the booze. And the sickness. And the long hard death. But I couldn't ever tell him anything past that. About the house. About the bottle caps. The books. The magazines. About myself. The junk that I lived with, that I could not live without. I told him that nobody else had been in my house since my dad died and I didn't feel ready yet and he said okay and then we made out on my porch because my neighbors probably couldn't see that far anyways and also because I didn't know them and didn't care what they thought.

Once at the fair Jared spent twenty dollars winning me a stuffed bear from the skee-ball game and I saw the bear in his arms and all the joy oozing out of him onto the bear making it sweet and sticky with good intent. I felt the evil, hungry thing growing inside of me, the want of whatever warmth had grown in his arms. I watched his face change from pride to horror as I began to cry right there in the light of the funnel cake stand. When I said I didn't want to talk about it Jared said okay and he called me the next day like nothing had happened.

I spent a lot of time at Jared's apartment. He lived on the other side of town in a renovated duplex that was much nicer than my house anyways. Except he didn't have a backyard for barbecuing and he had a daughter who had a summer birthday.

So one night, I told him. I said Jared there's something you need to know or maybe you need to see. And I walked him through every room in the house, the living room with its inflatable circus, the kitchen with its stockpile of novelty dishes and lava lamps, the bedrooms with their soft nests of books, magazines, newspapers, stuffed animals, the bathtub overflowing with cookie jars. And the garage. The sea of bottle caps, endlessly enticing, undulating under the dull glow of the naked overhead bulb. And then I took him out into the backyard and I laid down on the grass and he laid down next to me.

"I know I should've told you. And I know you probably don't want anything to do with me anymore. But, even if you don't want anything else to do with me, you could use my backyard for Jude's birthday party."

Jared didn't say anything for a while, he just rubbed my knuckles with his thumb. Then he turned over onto his side and smiled at me really big.

"We should have a garage sale. A huge one. You can xerox posters at the library and we can make it a whole event."

So the next weekend I set up the little kiddie pool I had bought for dad, and Jared brought Jude over in her floaties and she splashed around while we started on the house. We had just made it into the first bedroom when we heard a crashing sound from the garage. We ran in and found Jude practically convulsing, her face a dark purple. I called the ambulance while Jared tried to perform the Heimlich. I quickly handed Jared the phone and we switched roles. I looked down Jude's tiny little throat and realized her airway was blocked. I pushed two fingers down and yanked. It wasn't pretty, but it got the job done. We all cried a little bit until the ambulance arrived and the paramedics started checking on Jude.

"So what was it? That she swallowed?" I nearly jumped as Jared grabbed my shoulders. I didn't know what to say, so I just pulled the bottle cap out of my back pocket and gave it to him. I didn't know how to apologize. I didn't know how to explain. Nobody blamed me but I didn't need them to tell me that it was my fault.

That night, alone, I walked the garbage bags of bottle caps to the trash can and back for an hour and a half. I wanted them gone so bad, but at the same time, I didn't know how to remember myself without them. Eventually, I passed out on top of them in the living room, the soreness the next morning an apt punishment for my crimes. I called Jared. I told him I didn't know if I could see him anymore. I was scared. I didn't think I was ready. I wasn't used to people in my life, I was used to bottle caps and inflatable palm trees. But I wanted to be. I want to be.

* * *

This story first appeared in the After Dinner Conversation—November 2024 issue.

Discussion Questions

1. Is the term for what the narrator is going through grief, or is there another term that more aptly describes her experience? Is there a right and wrong way to react after the death of a loved one?

2. Why do you think the death of the narrator's father affected her so much? Why does the death of some parents seem to hit harder for certain people?

3. How do you know when it is healthy (*or unhealthy*) to keep a reminder of an experience or a person? What are examples of unhealthy keepsakes and healthy keepsakes? Are there examples of each in your own life?

4. How is keeping a bottle cap different than, or the same as, keeping a photo to remember a person? How do you know if you are remembering someone in an unhealthy way?

5. Could you continue a relationship with a hoarder after seeing their house overflowing with stuff? What, if anything, is the distinction between this issue, and others?

* * *

Disconnect

Julia Meinwald

* * *

Content Disclosure: Sexual Situations; Strong Language

* * *

It's 7:12 p.m., and Simone has this guy in the palm of her proverbial hand. Technically speaking, it's not her hand. The guy is on a date with Alexis, one of Simone's most loyal clients at Connect2. Simone is clicked into her terminal three miles away. Alexis has flipped the switch, giving Simone full control over her actions and words and full access to her thoughts and sensations. Each client feels different to pilot. If the client has joint pain or a headache, the pilot feels it. Many pilots find their first week on the job an almost spiritual experience, feeling the similarities and differences in how various human bodies move through the world. Simone, one of the most respected, in-demand pilots at Connect2, has inhabited over two hundred people.

Piloting Alexis is fun for Simone. Alexis has the sharpest sense of smell Simone has ever encountered, and her near-constant pulse of nervous energy feels energizing to Simone. Alexis is a well-oiled Porsche, and Simone is a racecar driver. Or something. Simone doesn't really care about cars, but Alexis has some strong memories associated with her father's prized Maserati. It's not Simone's job to unpack this. It's her job to make this guy fall for Alexis.

It doesn't hurt that Alexis is beautiful. She's gorgeous in a predictable blonde and leggy way. She has a nice laugh, too, which Simone deploys now to show this guy that she gets his Vonnegut reference. Simone hasn't actually read Vonnegut, but she knows enough to recognize popular characters and ideas. Guys never want to talk about the books anyway. They just want to throw down the reference to see if their date picks it up. "You're funny," she says to the guy. This is a bit on the nose for Simone, but she's calculated right; the guy preens and, as if repaying a social debt, asks her about herself. Or rather, he asks her about Alexis. Or, rather, he asks "Alexis" about Alexis.

If Alexis were in control right now, she would demur. She can't stand talking about herself and honestly finds a question as broad as "Tell me about yourself" borderline aggressive. Simone, however, has no problem with this. In her own life, she can happily monologue about the flurry of worries and amusements filling any given day. It's only slightly more difficult to do this for someone else. She tells the guy about the book Alexis is reading, about Alexis's sister's impending wedding, and transitions seamlessly into a story about a business lunch that draws attention to the impressive company where Alexis works in HR. She's careful to speak in Alexis's syntax. The less successful pilots at Connect2 go too far, making their clients perfect embodiments of charm. When the client flips the switch back and tries to take over, the discrepancies are glaring, and the subsequent dates are disastrous. Connect2 estimates that close to fifteen percent of first dates in Los Angeles involve a pilot, but getting caught as a passenger on a date is still considered a red flag in the dating world. The trick is to present Alexis as faithfully as possible—just amping up a few parameters to make a better first impression.

Simone has just revealed where Alexis went to college, and the guy makes a face that both women read as patronizing. Simone feels Alexis's impulse to flinch, but she stifles it. She pauses for a moment to see if Alexis is going to signal that she'd like to take control of the date, but she doesn't. Generally, clients flip the switch to take control mid-date in two situations: when they want to end the date prematurely or when they want to get physical. Every now and then, Simone gets someone who wants her to pilot the first kiss, but anything beyond that is forbidden by the Connect2 code of conduct. In Alexis and Simone's first few months together, Alexis would constantly flip the emergency override switch—forcibly seizing control against Simone's advice. A guy teasingly mocks her order? Emergency override. A guy doesn't get Simone-as-Alexis's funny joke? Uber is en route. After enough dates like this, though, Simone has earned Alexis's trust.

This guy seems judgmental, but Simone has gotten some positive bio-signals from Alexis. Part of Simone's job is to debrief with Alexis after the dates. To help her clarify her own feelings about a guy and choose a course of action. The consulting part is fun, but what Simone loves most are the dates themselves. Some of her friends think that piloting is like a superpower, but in truth, it's easier to see (and be) what someone else wants when you don't have to tend to your own personal desires. A surprising number of pilots at Connect2, including Simone, are single.

"I'm honestly shocked how many girls I go on dates with who just *don't read*," the guy is saying.

"Okay," says Simone, "I could be wrong, but is that tattoo on your wrist a literary reference?"

* * *

The day after the date is Alexis's twenty-ninth birthday. She knows it's not a big deal birthday. Next year, she might force herself to throw some sort of party for the big three-O. To pick the best, quietest, quirkiest bar in Silverlake, spend twelve hours crafting the perfect three-sentence email invite, then despair when only ten people show up and no one stays past midnight. Probably, though, she won't. Alexis doesn't act, she reacts. She receives, she waits, she happily makes the second move. It's a safer, easier way to move through the world.

Alexis doesn't list her birthday on social media, but it still feels like a personal affront that she's only gotten a handful of birthday greetings so far. None of them feel at all personal to her. She's got messages from her parents and her sister on the family text chain, but those feel rote, too. Alexis can't help but read this as a referendum on the quality of her personality. If she were smarter, funnier, kinder, she would probably be surrounded by gifts, confetti, and people who love her.

Her twenty-eighth birthday wasn't bad. Her boyfriend at the time took her to dinner, but just at their local Italian place, which had paper napkins and fewer cheese and pepper flake shakers than tables; the wait staff would ferry them back and forth between diners as needed. They talked, as they usually did, about his fantasy hockey league and how unethical and stupid various politicians were. The quotidian quality of the date made Alexis wonder if he was planning on dumping her. A few months later, he did indeed end things; Alexis was never sure if the lackluster birthday dinner was an early warning sign or not.

In an effort to celebrate herself (something culture seems to want her to do), Alexis takes a cupcake from her fridge and a birthday card from work out of her bag. All her coworkers have signed it, but the closest thing to a personalized message is the drawing of a rat wearing a party hat that her colleague Meredith drew in the card's lower right-hand corner. Meredith draws *Birthday Rat* on everyone's cards, but at least it has more personality than the usual "Happy birthday" and "Hope you have a fantabulous day!"

Her doorbell rings as she's stoically waiting for her cupcake to warm up and lose that cold fridge feeling. She springs to the door with an embarrassing dose of optimism. She's greeted by an old Asian woman bearing two dozen roses, which Alexis signs for and brings to the kitchen with cumbersome happiness. The card informs her that the roses are from Connect2. She's disappointed that they are from a company and not a person, but she has to admire their customer service.

Alexis suspects she's probably one of Connect2's most active users. She had hated dating before, but dates piloted by Simone are fun, and the debriefs are even better. Sometimes Alexis even accepts a date with a guy she knows she's not interested in, just so she can make fun of him with Simone after the fact.

Alexis's phone dings. It's an email from Simone listing

twenty-four things to love about Alexis—one for each rose in the bouquet. Alexis lifts the cupcake to her lips, reading the list again and again with each chocolaty bite.

* * *

Alexis shows up twelve minutes early for her debrief with Simone, sits in her car until she is only four minutes early, then enters the Connect2 building. The door to Simone's office is open, and Simone has implanted herself into a beanbag chair with two coffee mugs in front of her. Alexis lowers herself into the other beanbag as Simone exclaims, "Girl! You're wearing the sweater!" Simone and Alexis spent a good ten minutes going over the pros and cons of purchasing a turtleneck, debating whether Alexis could pull it off, and delving into what the larger ramifications of such a sartorial choice might be. Alexis shrugs with some pleasure.

"It looks so good!" says Simone. "You look like a stylish bunny rabbit. Can I touch it?"

Alexis nods, and Simone runs her hand down the length of Alexis's arm. To Alexis, it feels like the kinesthetic equivalent of ASMR. "Mmmmm," says Simone. "Softness."

"This is my first time wearing it," says Alexis.

"I'm honored I get to see it on its maiden voyage!" says Simone. "So, obviously, we have an agenda, but can I tell you a story first?"

"Always," says Alexis, settling into her beanbag.

"Okay, so I had an intro session with a new client yesterday. A really rich guy who just decided to open his marriage and wants to find a new sidepiece, these are his words, 'as efficiently as possible.' So, we finish up the regular intake stuff, and then he asks me... if I'll cut his hair."

"What?" Alexis laughs.

"Yeah, I was like, my dude, that is not part of this service, but best of luck to you."

"I might have done it," says Alexis, picking up the mug Simone has set out for her and inhaling deeply.

"Do you know how to cut hair?" asks Simone.

"A little. I cut some friends' hair in college. I've always thought there's something kind of romantic about it. In the right context, I mean. Something about how they trust you. It's like you're doing a loving act of service."

"Plus, you're kind of molding the person into a new version of themselves. New do, new you."

"Right. Like in those spy shows where the woman gets a new haircut and suddenly no one recognizes her."

Simone laughs. "So, shall we discuss our first order of business? Thumbs up or thumbs down on our Great Literary Mind?"

Alexis does a sideways thumb, and Simone lets out a theatrical groan. "Alexis!" she says. "They can't all be sideways thumbs! Seriously, is there *any* chance *this guy* is your soulmate?"

"There's a chance this coffee is my soulmate," says Alexis, making the kind of joke Simone makes and liking how it tastes in her mouth.

* * *

Simone clicks into her terminal for Alexis's next first date, and when she sees who the date is with, she almost chokes. Alexis is on a date with Jason. Neurotic, goofy, charming Jason. It's not unheard of for pilots to encounter someone they know in real life while on the job. The Connect2 code of conduct doesn't forbid it; you just need to fill out an extra form disclosing your situation. Simone knows immediately she will not be truthful when she fills out the form about Jason. She has harbored what could only be referred to as a tragic crush on him for close to two years. Members of the same running club, they often fall into pace with each other, and have even grabbed breakfast together after their runs on occasion. Simone has hinted pretty aggressively that she is interested, but Jason, a paragon of tact, has never acknowledged her overtures. He's perfected his Friend Face—a look that says *I adore you, but nothing interests me less than seeing you naked.*

Simone as Alexis goes through the basic opening pleasantries with Jason, asking about his day and how he chose this place. She is always invested in getting a good outcome for her clients, but for the first time, she feels nervous. It's strange seeing Jason in date mode. His hair is still wet from a shower, and she's never seen this plaid shirt before. She feels a strange mixture of jealousy and titillation.

"There's this painting," Jason says. "I don't know the name of it or who painted it, but it's of this woman in a field, sort of looking over her shoulder at the painter or at someone. It's weird, but I keep thinking you look just like that woman in the painting."

"Where did you see the painting?" she asks.

"I had a postcard of it in my room growing up," Jason answers.

"I had postcards in my room, too!" She gets a quizzical burst from Alexis, who never collected postcards. Simone doesn't think including this one personal detail from her own life will blow the facade. She has never felt this tight, focused kind of energy from Jason before. There's no harm in enjoying it for a moment.

"I'm so afraid of rambling on and sucking all the oxygen out of the room," says Jason. "Tell me about yourself." Simone goes through her basic intro-to-Alexis spiel. Jason asks if she wants to stay for another cup of coffee. Simone does.

* * *

The next day, after a 5K, the whole running group goes out drinking. Simone and Jason are sharing a massive plate of nachos, the bar is playing one of Simone's favorite albums in its entirety, and life is good. Even though she knows she did not actually go on a date with Jason the day before, she feels closer to him. She shifts her weight under the table, rubbing her toe up the leg of Jason's jeans. He stands abruptly, saying the next round is on him. Their friend Diane approaches and starts talking about whether or not she should quit her job. Simone looks to the bar, catches Jason's eye, and he makes a face at her like *we know the same thing*. She knows it's not a great sign that when she flirts with him, he pulls away, but her gin and tonic is delicious, and she is invincible. Jason sits back down with Simone and Diane, and the three of them go over the few pros and numerous cons of her job.

"Simone, you like *your* job, right?" slurs Diane.

"Being a professional Cyrano?" teases Jason. "Who wouldn't like that? Simone gets paid to date."

"And I get glowing reviews," Simone preens. "Promoted three times in as many years, *and* my picture is on our recruiting pamphlet."

"The face of the faceless," Jason says.

"Let's play a game," says Simone. "Everyone think of a secret about the person to your left and whisper it to the person to your right." She leans close to Jason and whispers, "There's someone at this table I want to kiss more than Diane."

Jason smirks and bonks Simone on the top of her head. "Good secret, drunko." He leans over to Diane and whispers, loud enough for Simone to hear, "Simone has two levels, totally sober and totally wasted. Nothing in between."

Diane leans into Simone and whispers, "I fucking *hate* my job." She has not fully understood the assignment.

They stay out until closing, and Simone and Jason are the last two standing on the curb, waiting for their Ubers. Simone keeps reaching for Jason's hand, and he keeps holding it for a few seconds, then letting it go.

"I think you're just the cat's meow," says Simone. Then, taking his hand again, "I'm not tired yet."

"Simone. Not tonight," says Jason.

A minute or so later, his Uber shows up, and he gets in. Simone knows rejection when she hears it. But she can't help coming back to the possibilities that all non-tonight nights might still hold.

* * *

Simone is still feeling cocktails four through six from the night before when she meets Alexis for their next check-in. Alexis is paying three dollars a minute to meet with her, wrapped into her monthly bill, but Simone often gives her an extra ten minutes or so for free because Alexis is one of the sane ones. Simone genuinely would like to see a happy ending for her.

"For me, Jason is a pass," Alexis says, once they've briefly compared notes on the previous night's episode of *The Bachelor*. "He was so in his head. I felt like we were both so nervous; it was hard for me to get comfortable."

Simone is genuinely surprised. It's hard to picture someone not liking Jason. "To be fair," says Simone, "you don't usually feel comfortable when first meeting someone."

"I didn't take an official tally," Alexis says, "but I think he apologized to me, like, ten times over one coffee." Simone guffaws.

"Yeah, he did seem pretty eager to impress," says Simone. "If you want, next time I can keep an official 'I'm sorry' count from my terminal. We can make an over/under bet, and if you win, I'll let you give me a haircut."

"I think if I win, you should give *me* a haircut," says Alexis.

"You may find the results alarming, but yes, I'm in," says Simone, shaking Alexis's hand.

"So, you really think I should see him again?" asks Alexis.

"Has he reached out to you?" Simone asks, trying not to sound overly invested.

"He asked if I'm up for dinner on Friday," Alexis confirms.

"Tell him yes," says Simone.

* * *

Getting dressed for her second date with Jason, Alexis is thinking about soulmates. As part of the intake process at Connect2, clients have to describe how they picture their soulmate. Most people jot down a few sentences about being someone's priority or feeling sparks that mature into smoldering embers. Alexis wrote close to a thousand words. Alexis thinks a soulmate is someone who knows all of your thoughts and still accepts you. She thinks a soulmate gives you small doses of optimism when you can't get out of your own head. She thinks things that are hard for you will be easy for your soulmate. Where Alexis is shy, her soulmate will have chutzpah. Things that Alexis fears will be welcome challenges for her soulmate. Simone, trying to lighten the mood, proclaims all sorts of people and things to be her soulmate: the deli cat next door to Connect2's offices, the writer of that one SNL sketch that was actually really good, comfortable shoes, a nice breeze. The message, Alexis thinks, is that her soulmate might be right under her unusually sensitive nose. Alexis thinks Simone may be right about this.

* * *

When Simone clicks in for Alexis and Jason's dinner date, she sees that Alexis has not even worn one of her top ten date outfits, but Jason is looking sweaty and serious in a way that Simone finds lovely.

"I've got you," Simone says to Alexis, as she always does right before she flips the switch to take control. "This is going to be a good night."

* * *

Over dinner, Jason asks Alexis question after question. He asks if she can hear him chewing (she can), if she has ever gotten so mad she's wanted to hit someone (she hasn't), if she thinks David Lynch is going to make any more films (she doesn't care). As Simone's words come out of her mouth, though, Alexis realizes that Simone cares. She cares about David Lynch films; she teases Jason with a warmth Alexis doesn't feel. Alexis learns more about Simone on this date than in all of their debriefs together.

Alexis lets her mind wander, thinking about how strange being piloted is. She smells the flowers Jason has brought her, thinking *I am letting Simone smell flowers.* She raises her hand to her cheek. *Simone is touching my face. Simone tastes the sweet whipped cream I'm swallowing.* Simone has access to these thoughts, but is focused on the guy sitting across from Alexis.

The check comes, and Jason looks down. "So, I don't know if you'd want to, I dunno, go for a walk or maybe come to my place for a drink?" he says.

* * *

Simone has seen Alexis's engagement drifting as dinner has worn on, but she feels like she's on one of the best dates of her life. Especially when the conversation turns philosophical, and she can push aside Alexis's biographical specifics and share more of her own views. When she makes Jason laugh, she feels like a queen.

Simone doesn't see what harm a quick postprandial walk could do. She gets that Alexis isn't attracted to Jason, but she hasn't flipped the switch to take control and end the date.

"You live near here?" Simone asks as Alexis, knowing that he does.

"Just a couple blocks away." Jason smiles.

It has rained, leaving the air cool and the streets glistening. They cut across a park and, in a few minutes, arrive at Jason's building. Simone tries to soak in each second, knowing that Alexis will take control and end the date at any moment.

"God. I can't get over how beautiful you are," says Jason. Then he kisses her. It's a kiss Simone has been thinking about for over a year, and just the fact of it finally happening is mind-blowing. She kisses him back.

* * *

Alexis does not like kissing this loud-chewing, ever-apologizing guy. His lips feel gummy against hers. She's fascinated, though, by the idea that both she and Simone are in the same kiss. How strange, she thinks, to be a conduit for someone else's pleasure. Jason's hands are all over her now. His touches are all too gentle like he's trying to tickle her. Meanwhile, Simone is using Alexis's hands in ways she never would. She's pulling handfuls of Jason's hair, biting his lips. Alexis concentrates on being there but not there. She imagines herself as the spoke of a wheel, perfectly still, warmly wrapped in the embrace of perpetual motion.

* * *

Here are the things Simone most likes remembering from her night with Jason. The way that he put his hand between her head and the backboard of his bed so she wouldn't bang it against the wood. The fact that after taking off her blouse, Jason folded it and put it on his nightstand. Sure, it's not her blouse, not her head, but the experience was immersive. Her favorite memory is the few seconds of silence after they'd slept together, broken by Jason saying, with a goofy smile, "So, that was fun." Alexis hadn't flipped the switch until they'd finished coffee and a crossword the next morning.

She knows that if her supervisor digs into the logs for this date, it won't be good. Alexis's biodata didn't align with the choices Simone was making for her, and Simone has violated a clear rule against piloting a sexual encounter. Technically, it's a fireable offense, possibly even one with legal consequences. She's confident, though, that if Alexis really wanted to take back control, she would have. Maybe, Simone thinks, Alexis was even giving her some sort of gift—intuited Simone's investment in the moment and decided not to take it away from her. Simone knows she's done something wrong, but until an outside party tells her how wrong, she's going to assume the transgression was minor.

* * *

That Sunday, Simone sits across from Jason, digging into diner eggs after a run. Simone keeps trying to steal potatoes off Jason's plate, and Jason keeps pushing her fork away.

"What's up with you this morning?" Simone finally asks.

"It's nothing," says Jason. Then, after an uncharacteristic silence between them, "I kinda get the feeling that you don't love it when I talk about my romantic life."

"That's crazy. You can talk to me about anything."

"Okay. Well, I guess I'm in a funk because I went on what I thought was a really great date with this girl, but she ghosted me."

Simone fills her lungs with courage. "I mean, I know I'm not this amazing girl who ghosted you, but *I'd* be pretty into taking you on a date sometime." Jason looks at his eggs. Too many seconds pass. "Maybe a romantic trapeze lesson?" she appends lamely.

Finally, Jason arranges his features into Friend Face. "You're such a loon," he says, taking a forkful of potatoes and plopping them onto Simone's plate. "Eat your eggs and stop prying into my sad love life." Simone has been drunk on the great flood of serotonin coursing through her ever since the date. Here, in this overbright diner, rejected once again, she crashes hard. They finish breakfast in relative quiet, both thinking back to their own separate versions of the same night.

* * *

Alexis brings macaroons to her Monday session with

Simone. For some reason, she wonders if Simone will bring some kind of confection herself—if they will be faced with an embarrassment of desserts—but when she arrives, Simone is empty-handed, slumped in her beanbag.

"So," Alexis begins, "crazy date, huh?"

Simone smiles weakly, then seems to resolve to engage and sits up a bit straighter. "I counted twelve on the apology tally, so I think I owe you a haircut," says Simone, but her eyes aren't fully smiling. The excitement Alexis had felt on the drive over starts to evaporate. It's not that she'd imagined passionately kissing Simone. She hadn't even imagined Simone thanking her. She'd just pictured the two of them sipping coffee and dissecting their shared experience.

"I don't think there's going to be a third date with Jason," she says carefully.

"Well, you can't force yourself to be into someone you're just not into," says Simone. Alexis wonders if Simone is referring to her own disdain for Alexis. She wonders if Simone thinks she is pathetic. To be rejected by someone who is literally paid to spend time with her would be a new low.

Meeting with Alexis usually energizes Simone, but today even Alexis's open face, her receptivity to all Simone has to offer, isn't enough. Simone knows what Alexis wants from her, abstractly at least. If she was piloting someone else in her shoes, she would give Alexis a hug, tell her the date had been wild and she'd never done anything like that before. Tell Alexis that she'd love to get dinner sometime, just the two of them. As both pilot and passenger, Simone can't get any of this out.

"What're all these boxes for?" Alexis asks.

"Well, my friend, it's the end of an era," says Simone.

"Today is my last day at Connect2."

"Oh, did you...."

"My manager reviewed the logs from your date with Jason."

"Weren't you pilot of the month last month?"

Simone is briefly impressed with Alexis's memory. "Yeah, for the third time. But, they take the code of conduct seriously."

"I wasn't... I would have taken back control if... I mean, I think it was an interesting night for everyone." Alexis can't quite articulate why she let things go so far. It has something to do with the overfull sensation of being touched by one person while your thoughts stream to someone else. It has something to do with grasping for the only kind of connection you can reach.

"Being a star employee was sort of *my thing,*" says Simone. "But, at the end of the day, I'm just a girl who gets fired for cause. Anyway, I guess they'll assign you a different pilot."

"I don't really want another pilot."

"Yeah," Simone sighs, with a roll of her eyes. "I'm basically irreplaceable." She takes a half-hearted bite of the macaroon Alexis brought. "These are good. You didn't have to do this."

"Oh, I know," says Alexis. "I wanted to." Then, reaching shyly into her bag, "I brought something else." Alexis pulls out a hairbrush and a simple pair of cutting scissors. She guides Simone from the beanbag to a proper chair, spreading an old sheet she brought from home on the floor around them. She smooths Simone's hair. She runs her fingers across Simone's scalp. She brushes out Simone's wild mane until it is a cloud around her head. She begins to cut.

"New do, new you, right?"

Simone feels herself relax, if only a little. She tries to breathe out Jason, breathe out her manager's disappointment, and breathe in the feeling of Alexis's hands at work. To embrace the idea that a macaroon and the friend who brings it to you is a thing of great value.

"This haircut is my soulmate," Simone says. She's not entirely wrong.

* * *

This story first appeared in the After Dinner Conversation—May 2024 issue.

Discussion Questions

1. If you could have someone "pilot" you on a date, would you allow them to? At what point in the date would you want to take over control? After how many dates would you no longer want them to pilot you? Would you ever tell your partner you were piloted at the start of the relationship?

2. Is there a difference between being "piloted" by another person on a date and being the date version of yourself on a date? (*energetic, interested, funny...*) If so, what is the difference in presenting these two false versions of yourself?

3. Connect2 asks clients to describe how they picture their soulmate. How would you describe your soulmate? To be truly happy in a relationship, must a person date their imagined soulmate? Is a person settling for less if they date someone who doesn't exactly meet those ideals?

4. Given that Alexis could take back control at any time, did Simone do anything wrong by continuing the date through sexual intercourse?

5. If you could, like Simone and Alexis, share the experience and sensations of a sexual encounter with someone else, would you? Who would you share that experience with? Would you be obligated to tell your partner two minds inhabited the one body in front of them?

* * *

Emancipation

Darcy Alvey

* * *

<u>**Content Disclosure**</u>: None

* * *

A plate of meat loaf and mashed potatoes balanced on her knees, Lorene watched a National Geographic documentary about a fifty-something woman living utterly alone on the tundra north of the Arctic circle, her home a compound of metal storage containers. An aerial shot showed open land in every direction, unmarred by roads or telephone poles or any life force other than the terns and puffins crossing overhead, the occasional white-tailed eagle, and alpha predators like polar bears, wolverines, and musk ox.

Lorene scooted closer to hear better. If she adjusted the volume, Frank might come out of his den and spoil the moment. She forgot to eat as she watched the woman survive a white-out blizzard, tethering herself to a pole to reach supplies in another building. The storm, biblical in its ferocity, lasted three days and three nights. After it cleared, the woman walked outside to find her refueling outpost on the edge of nowhere, all but buried in drifted snow. Overturned oil drums had been scattered across the yard by the force of the wind. Her greenhouse, prepared days earlier for spring planting, lay in tatters, its door banging in the leftover breeze. Even the sky, the color of watered-down milk, looked spent by the mayhem.

"Mother Nature, you got me good this time," the woman yelled to the heavens, "but I'm still here."

That was when Lorene decided to end her marriage. The idea of leaving Frank had been brewing for some time. Through the last years, they had stopped sharing the small details of everyday life, even stopped eating meals together, he carting his plate to his workroom, she sitting in front of the television or reading at the kitchen table. They split the chores. He did the grocery shopping, she the cooking. He took out the trash, she mowed the small back lawn. Saturday nights, if both were home, they had sexual relations. It had all become very cordial.

Lorene knew they could continue their current path indefinitely. Maybe that was the problem, nothing to look forward to other than more of the same. A few weeks earlier, their thirty-fourth wedding anniversary had come and gone. Getting ready for bed the night before, Lorene had suggested dinner at The Roundup to mark the occasion, but that turned out to be the night of Frank's monthly stamp club meeting. Neither suggested an alternate date.

Her mind filled with mushing huskies and seaplanes skidding on frozen rivers as Lorene tidied the kitchen and headed for bed. On her way, she grabbed *Call of the Wild* from the bookcase in Ruby's old room. She quickly lost herself in the story of Buck, the splendid Saint Bernard, and the Klondike gold strike of the late 1800s. How enticing it all sounded. Wasn't it Jack London who said something about living full-out versus merely existing?

At ten sharp, Frank started his nightly rounds. Lorene heard him check that the outside doors were locked, the windows closed and latched. From there, he headed to the hallway to set the thermostat at sixty-five before coming up the stairs. The banality of it all struck her when he walked into the room. Her husband had always liked his routine. When they were first married, she had thought it endearing the way he organized everything down to the spice cupboard in the kitchen and the catchall utensil drawer. He looked to see her there but didn't say anything. She watched him ready himself for bed, hang his shirt and pants in the closet, place his shoes side by side on the little rack, take his pajamas from the top dresser drawer. He was still trim, with only a slight bulge of the stomach from a taste for malt whiskey. His hair had thinned. She used to like running her fingers through it. Now he kept it so short she could see his scalp. Like clockwork, he headed to the bathroom to take his cholesterol pill and brush his teeth. Rinse and spit. Rinse and spit.

"I'm going grocery shopping tomorrow," he called from the bathroom. Doubtless, he was combing his hair. "Is there anything you want?"

"Bananas." She hated yelling from room to room.

"Bananas? That's it?" he yelled back.

She didn't answer.

"My legs have been cramping," she said when he returned.

"Bananas have potassium, good for leg cramps," he said.

"I know, Frank. That's why I asked for bananas."

"Just trying to help." He squinched his mouth, indicating he was annoyed with her.

Frank never came out and said he was peeved. Instead, he made sarcastic remarks that scored tiny wounds. If she complained, he said she couldn't take a joke.

Facing away from her, he started his calisthenics drill. Beginning at the top of his head, he proceeded muscle by muscle down his body, twisting and stretching, groaning with pleasure or pain, she wasn't sure which.

"I started rereading *Call of the Wild*," she said as he lunged forward and then back to upright.

He didn't turn around. "Jack London? I have a Jack London stamp, you know. Part of the Great American series. Sixty-four honorees, all headshots. I'm only missing Alice Paul and Hap Arnold."

"Are you happy, Frank?"

He finished touching his toes and turned to look at her. "What kind of question is that? Am I happy? Find me a Hap Arnold, and I'll be happy."

She shrugged. "I'm serious. Would you consider yourself happy? That's all I'm asking."

"I don't think about it."

"Well, I don't think I am, Frank. Happy. Not at this moment in time, anyway."

He looked bewildered. "What does that mean? Didn't you just get the new couch you wanted?"

"There's more to life than couches, Frank. We've got this one life, and there's a whole world out there. Remember when we wanted to join the Peace Corps and head to Africa? What happened to that dream?"

"That was always your dream, not mine. I'm good right where I am." He climbed into bed and turned on the news. The sexy weatherwoman forecast a storm for the next few days.

Over the noise of the television, Lorene listened to the dull hum of traffic from the freeway a couple of blocks away. People were going places.

"Anything else for the grocery list? I'm not going twice."

"Leftover meat loaf for dinner tomorrow," she said. "Get something to go with that if you want."

"We need catsup." Frank jotted catsup below bananas in a little binder he kept next to the bed. "The meat loaf was a little dry."

"Dry?" Lorene said. "Dry." She made meat loaf from scratch, the way her grandmother taught her, with minced onions, a raw egg, homemade breadcrumbs, a dash of milk, Worcestershire sauce—and catsup.

"Get something else for dinner tomorrow if you want something else," she said. The first time she'd made meat loaf all those years ago, he'd said it was the best thing he ever ate.

"Leftover meat loaf is fine. Jesus."

Yanking the sheet to her chin, she turned away and closed her eyes.

At the end of the news, Frank switched off the television, laid his glasses on his nightstand, and reached to peck her on the cheek.

She pretended to be asleep.

* * *

The following morning, Lorene stayed in bed as Frank dressed for work. He kept the books for an insurance agency, adding and subtracting columns of numbers all day, making sure bills got paid on time. Frank could be counted on to keep things running smoothly. That was one of the things she had found attractive from the start. She'd needed that at the time. Before leaving the room, he snatched the shopping list off his nightstand with exaggerated vigor, glancing in her direction. Lorene made a face to his back. Pulling on her robe, she followed him to the kitchen.

"I'll get coffee at the office." He grabbed an apple and a granola bar and headed toward the back door. "I won't forget your bananas." His parting shot.

Lorene fired back, "Don't forget your catsup." Damn, she hated being petty.

She padded to the front window to watch him leave. When his car pulled away, she took a deep breath and glanced around the neighborhood. This had been home for, what, thirty-four years? Suddenly, it looked unfamiliar, like she hadn't seen it for a long time. Ruby had been little more than a toddler when they moved in. The pepper trees, planted by the developers, had long ago reached full height. Age had come on the neighborhood without her noticing. Weeds sprouted from the cracks in the asphalt street like wiry chin hairs. Many of the lawns had patchy spots run through by crabgrass. Some of the houses had been maintained; some retained only a nod to early dignity. Beyond the trees, the sky looked clear and wide, a good omen for new starts.

Enjoying the moment of quiet, she watched Old Man Bitters jog by, his rate of travel more in time with a walk than a run. His face was red from the exertion, his arms pumped for all they were worth. Too heavy to be expending so much energy.

Still, Lorene appreciated his effort. Frank would have thought him foolish. Maybe he was, but at least he wasn't giving up.

A night's sleep had done nothing to change her mind about the divorce. If anything, she was more certain with each passing moment. She would tell Frank right away. If she waited, she might lose her courage, the days slipping away one by one in an agony of indecision. She would break the news before she told Ruby. She owed him that. Tonight, after dinner, she would call him from his den for the powwow that would change both their lives.

She grabbed a pad and pencil and sat at the kitchen table to plan her getaway, which was how she had come to think of it. Frank would approve—her making notes about something. Figuring out how to support herself would come first. What could she do? She'd never worked outside the home, focusing on raising Ruby, cooking meals, dusting and dusting and dusting. She had earned a degree in geology, taking night classes at the local college; she'd done that for her dad in gratitude for all the times he'd taken her camping. They'd collected rock specimens, slept under the stars, and cooked over an open fire. She realized now it was the only entertainment he could afford, but she wouldn't have changed a moment of it. She wouldn't think about the other times after her mother died when her father disappeared for days without a word. Their neighbor Sheila would look in on her until he came home remorseful, promising to do better.

Throughout the afternoon, she searched the Internet for job openings, starting as far from home as she could get. If she was going to go, go big. That would be her new philosophy. Although she had no actual experience, she had the degree. A position for a geologist at Parc National de l'Ankarana in Madagascar was surely far enough away. The underground rivers looked breathtaking in the photos, a hidden world just below the Earth's surface. Cal Orko in Bolivia needed a lab assistant. How amazing would it be to study the prehistoric dinosaur footprints that ran along the sides of the rock outcrops? Or the Danakil Depression in Ethiopia, maybe something there. The thought of it all thrilled her like nothing had in a long time. She felt like a kid again.

* * *

At 5:30, Lorene opened a can of peas as Frank pulled into the drive. Without a word, he dropped the bananas and catsup on the counter and headed to his den. His snub shouldn't have hurt, but it did. When everything was heated through, she called him to dinner. He didn't come right away.

"The food's getting cold," she said when he finally strolled into the kitchen.

If he heard the pique in her voice, he ignored it. "I was in the middle of something."

"You're always in the middle of something."

He picked up his plate and snagged the bottle of catsup, ready to head back to his cave.

"Let's eat in the dining room," she said.

He turned back at the door. "But I'm halfway through cataloging my American Philosophers series."

"For once, let's have dinner together."

Did he roll his eyes?

"Does it have to be the dining room? Why not here in the kitchen?" He started to put his plate on the little table under the window.

"Yes, it has to be in the dining room. It's all set up."

Earlier, Lorene had laid out cloth placemats and coordinating napkins on their large walnut table, deciding her big announcement deserved a degree of formality—to underscore its importance. They took places at opposite ends of the table.

"Aren't we fancy," Frank said.

Lorene watched him drown his meat loaf in catsup after scraping his vegetables to the side. He started eating right away as if he didn't plan on staying long. She sipped from her water goblet and moved her vegetables around the plate.

He looked up to see her staring at him. "What's with the fancy setup?" he said. "Did I forget your birthday or something?"

"Ha-ha." By some cosmic coincidence, she and Frank shared the same date of birth—August 5.

She speared a pea. It was so clear he'd rather be elsewhere fiddling with his stamps, gloating over his latest find.

Frank filled the chilly silence. "When was the last time we ate in here, anyway?"

Although they didn't use it often, the dining room was Lorene's favorite part of the house. Growing up in a trailer with only her father, she had dreamed about a two-story home populated with children, a place with a dining room large enough for everyone to gather and share their day. Ruby was a toddler when they moved in. Although she hadn't been able to have more children, Lorene covered the walls in paper with cheerful green vines on a white lattice background and hung an antique chandelier in the center of the ceiling. A large oval table found at Goodwill took up most of the floor space. Frank had always thought the room a waste; they used it so seldom. To her, it didn't matter how often they gathered there. It mattered that it existed.

"Our last meal here was Thanksgiving two years ago," she said, "right after my father died. Ruby flew in. Your parents brought a molded cranberry Jell-O and hammered you throughout dinner about not going to church."

"It's all coming back." He scratched his nearly bald head.

Lorene waited to speak as Frank started in on his peas. He slouched in his chair, elbows on the table. All those meals alone in his den had cost him his table manners. Had he shrunk in the last few years? His skin seemed loose on his five-ten frame. She wanted to tell him to sit up straight, like his mother would have had she been there.

"We need to have a talk," she said.

The clock on the old oak sideboard sounded the half hour with a loud bong, startling them both.

"Ask not for whom the bell tolls, eh, Lorene? Let's have it. What have I done now?"

"Really, Frank. That's where you go first? 'What have I done now?' This isn't about you."

"Well, it feels like it's about me." He buttered a slice of bread like he was frosting a cake.

Maybe he was right. She took a deep breath. "I'm just going to say it. I'm not happy. I haven't been happy for a while."

"Is that what you were going on about last night?"

"Yes, that's what I was going on about. I need to make a change in my life." The words came out in one puff of breath: "I want a divorce, Frank." There, she said it. It shocked her to verbalize the word after only thinking it for so long. Saying it out loud made it real.

Her husband dropped the last bite of bread on his plate and stared at her across the length of the table. "Divorce, Lorene? That's a little histrionic, don't you think?"

"Maybe histrionic. It's now or never, Frank. At fifty-two, I'm not getting any younger."

Just last week, she had discovered a streak of white hair over her right temple. And she tired more easily. While gardening, she had to pause every now and then to catch her breath. Even the mailman had remarked on her advancing age, calling her "ma'am" more than once. It added up. Clasping her hands in her lap, Lorene tried not to fidget. How was it he always made her feel like a child?

"Let's be real here," he said. "You're a person of extremes." He had the nerve to chuckle. "Remember the time you decided to become a rock climber? You watched videos. You checked out books at the library. You bought the gear. Correct me if I'm wrong, but there's still a box of rope and metal crampons in the garage. Then, one class at the rec center, and you realized you were afraid of heights."

"That's mean, Frank."

Warming to the subject, he made a pyramid with his hands. "And what about the time you decided to learn Russian? You wanted to take the train across Siberia, so you bought the learn-a-language-in-a-month video series. I haven't heard you conversing in Russian lately."

"Zho-pa. That's one word I learned. It means 'ass.' At least I try things. I know this is going to sound dramatic, and you hate that, but I want to set my own course for the first time in my life."

"Uh-huh. How exactly do you plan to do that? I don't see

how a degree in geology is going to get you very far, especially without a scintilla of experience."

"You'd be surprised. I've been searching the Internet, and there are quite a few entry-level openings for geologists, especially in third-world countries."

"You want to head to a third-world country for your first real job."

"Maybe I do. And it wouldn't be my first real job. I'd call taking care of you and Ruby and the house a real job."

"Come to think of it, I guess you could be a housekeeper. They probably need those in third-world countries."

"Zho-pa, Frank. You can be a real zho-pa."

"You're right. That was uncalled for. But there must be something besides chucking it all and heading off into the wilds of Uganda or wherever. What about trying yoga? Or getting a dog? Why not take a trip to visit Ruby in New York? You can tell her what a lousy husband I am. Speaking of which, have you told Ruby of your plan?

"I wanted to tell you first. I felt like I owed you that."

He dipped his head like a king to a vassal. "Thank you for the consideration."

With a sigh, she stood and switched on the overhead light. They had been bickering so long it was getting dark. Through the dangling shards of the chandelier, rays filtered down to make a snowflake pattern on the table.

"So, what's next? What's the big plan?" There was a tightness to his face now.

"I haven't figured out all the details, Frank. You're the one who always preaches 'one step at a time.'"

With that, he stood and dropped his napkin next to his

plate. "When you decide, let me know. I'll be in my den."

* * *

The next morning Lorene woke to rain. Frank was downstairs already, so she could revel in the downpour. The sound reminded her of her childhood when rain beat against the metal roof of their trailer, at times loud, at times slow and soft, according to the push of the wind. Smiling, she tapped her fingers on the bedsheet in accompaniment.

Buoyed enough to face Frank, she dressed in a sweatshirt and jeans and headed downstairs, grabbing her yellow slicker on the way. Like every other Saturday in living memory her husband sat at the kitchen table doing the crossword in the morning paper.

"There's coffee," he said without looking up.

He said it like the night before had never happened. She poured a cup and leaned against the cabinets, sipping, watching him scribble away at the puzzle without a care in the world.

"This should be right up your alley," he muttered before she said anything. "Geological plates. Eight letters."

She set her cup on the counter. "Do you even remember that I asked you for a divorce last night?"

He leaned back in his chair. "Of course I remember. I thought you were kidding or mad at me or something."

"Or something," she said, pulling on the slicker. "I'm going for a walk. I don't suppose you'd like to join me."

He glanced out the window. "It's raining."

"I realize. All the better."

"I'll pass," he said. "Don't blame me if you catch a cold. I speak with the wisdom of personal experience, if you recall."

"The illness to which you refer happened while we were

dating, some thirty-odd years ago. Maybe you could give it a second shot."

Early in their relationship, Lorene had cajoled Frank into a walk in the rain. It had been a warm summer evening, and she'd thought it romantic. "We can skip through the puddles and dance like Gene Kelly in *Singing in the Rain*," she'd offered as inducement. He gave in back then. The next day, as if decreed, he'd come down with a nasty head cold, keeping him in bed for days.

"Once was enough." He shook his head. "You go. Dance your heart out."

Back to his puzzle.

"Thank you, I will." She snapped the words as she headed for the door.

"Geez, you're in a mood. Don't expect me to take care of you when you get sick."

"My hero," she said from the doorway.

"Before you go: geological plates?"

"Look it up, Frank."

Lorene stood on the front porch for a long moment, slowing her breath. Everything about her husband irritated her these days. The way he ate his food, one item at a time to completion—meat, vegetables, starch, in that order. He hadn't always been that way. Although less adventurous, he'd been open to new things once upon a time, especially if they made her happy. What happened to that Frank? Was there an instant—a specific event—that made him so myopic now, or had the change come in small increments over time, like the gradual wearing away of sedimentary rock? In either case, he no longer resembled the man she married.

She stepped out onto the sidewalk. The air felt warm, the rain cleansing. Opening her mouth, she caught a drop on her tongue. Everything shimmered—the hawthorn bushes that hedged the side yard, the red bird feeder hanging in the pepper tree, the wet asphalt street gleaming like polished onyx. Even the cars parked along the curb shed the falling water like children under a lawn sprinkler. Heading off, Lorene stamped a puddle or two and relished the good splat. She followed a leaf as it flowed along the curb, walking at its pace until it disappeared down a storm drain. At the park where she had taken Ruby to swing as a child, she picked a yellow daisy to stick in her hair. She wasn't the only one enjoying the weather. Old Man Bitters jogged by as she paused at a corner. His step seemed springier than the last time, his face a rosy glow. The rain had taken ten years off his life. He waved, and she waved back.

Frank was finishing a bowl of bran flakes when she returned home. "You look like a drowned rat," he said.

"Thank you. I feel great." She dropped her wet umbrella in the sink.

"For now." He nodded sagely. "Tectonic, by the way—geological plates. I looked it up." He tapped the paper with a knuckle.

"Good for you, Frank. You get the gold star."

That night, in bed, Frank reached to rub her shoulder the way he did every Saturday, signaling his intention. It was the shorthand of a long marriage, the little two-step they had orchestrated over time. When he touched her in that way, Lorene would put down her book, marking the page, pull her nightgown over her head, and wait for him to crawl on top of her and pound away. It hadn't always been so clinical. In the early days, they couldn't get enough of each other. Public places had been especially thrilling, spots that offered the titillating prospect of getting caught in the act. Their first time had been on the minuscule patch of lawn behind the rec room of the trailer park. The next morning Lorene had discovered welts all over her backside from a small colony of red ants they'd been too busy to notice. Once, in the back seat of Frank's Volkswagen Bug at the drive-in movie theater, they'd climaxed while *Pee-Wee's Big Adventure* played on the giant screen. Tonight, Lorene shrank from his touch as if it burned her skin.

"Really, Frank, do you even care that I asked you for a divorce, or is that inconsequential to your needs?"

Frank fell back to his side of the bed. For the first time since she made her announcement, he got angry. "Haven't you played this game long enough? It's getting old."

Lorene grabbed her pillow and a quilt she kept at the foot of the bed. She looked at her husband and realized something. Over the years, he had winnowed his emotional and physical needs to the bare minimum necessary for survival. His days were filled with chores and obligations and his precious stamps. When was the last time she'd heard him laugh out loud? Did he ever sing when no one was listening or lie on the grass and make the clouds into dragons and sea monsters? He lived in a cocoon, warm and safe but without wonder.

"You've lost your joy in life, Frank. That's the problem. We've both lost our joy."

* * *

As the weeks went by, Lorene set her plan in motion. She applied for entry-level positions in geology, environmental studies, archaeology, anything remotely interesting. When not job hunting, she readied for her departure in other ways. She sorted cupboards, made trips to the Goodwill, set aside things for Ruby. She gathered boxes from behind the liquor store and packed the possessions she wanted to take with her—presents and cards from Ruby through the years, rocks gathered with her father, the geode Frank gave her for their tenth anniversary. Frank watched it all, shaking his head, making little jokes about everything she did. When she pulled the suitcases down from the hall closet, that seemed to be the last straw.

"Lorene, I just tripped over one of your suitcases at the foot of the bed."

She was watching television in the living room when he walked up behind her. The Arctic woman was skinning a bear that had ventured too close to her compound. "I've been telling you I'm serious, Frank."

"This is ridiculous. Use your head. You do realize you'll be competing with people half your age."

"Thanks for the reminder," she said. "Neither of us is getting any younger. Besides, I have wisdom that comes with age. That should count for something."

She could sense his breath on her neck. "Quit hovering behind me. If you want to talk, come sit down."

He rounded the couch and perched on the edge of a chair. "Let's get real, Lorene. Exactly how are you planning to finance this little adventure?"

"Last I checked, we live in a community-property state. Our assets get divided down the middle. My half of our savings will hold me over until everything is worked out."

That brought him up short. "You won't get half of my stamp collection, I'll tell you right now."

She almost laughed. A few days earlier, he bought a Hap Arnold in good condition from a collector in New Mexico and had been quietly gloating ever since. "Don't worry, you can have your stamps all to yourself."

"What does Ruby say? Have you told her of your big plan?"

"I did."

"And?"

"She said she'd support whatever decision I made."

"Did she say anything about what this would mean to me?"

"She said you're a big boy and will figure it out."

Unconsciously, he twisted his gold wedding band around on his finger. "I still don't get it. What happened to 'til death do us part' anyway? Didn't that mean anything?"

"You realize I was eighteen when I said those words. I still lived with my father. I'd barely gotten my braces off, for God's sake. How could I possibly know then what I was going to want for the rest of my life?"

She searched for the right words to explain something even she didn't fully understand. "I need to live without a safety net, Frank. Corny as it sounds, I need to depend on only myself for the first time in my life, to see what I'm made of. And what's so bad, since you ask, is the fun has gone out of everything. I can't remember the last time I got up in the morning excited about the day."

"And that's my fault?"

"No, it's my fault, and I'm the one that has to do something about it."

They sat in silence, each waiting for the other to speak.

Lorene snuck a peek at the television. The Arctic woman was gone, replaced by someone giving step-by-step instructions on how to cook a pasta dish.

When Frank spoke, he sounded sad. "I've tried to be a good husband, a good provider. I've been there for you through your emotional ups and downs. Have I abused you in any way? Have I ever stopped you from doing anything? Didn't I babysit Ruby while you took night classes at the college?"

"You don't babysit your own child, Frank. No, it's more than that. You're not the man I married. What happened to the guy who brought me flowers and surprised me with tickets to the opera even knowing you'd hate every minute of it? You've become negative. Your response to everything I suggest is a knee-jerk reaction—'no, no, no,' before you even let me finish. Do you know how disheartening that is? I have to give myself a pep talk before I ask you to do anything. Even if you change your mind later, by then, the excitement is gone, punctured like a party balloon. You wouldn't so much as walk with me in the rain. It's the little things, Frank, the small moments that make life worth living. I want to experience those full out. I can't do that staying here."

"Even if you didn't get sick, walking in the rain was plain ludicrous. You can't blame me for not going. No sane person would do that."

"So now I'm insane?"

"You know what I mean."

She sensed his pain but stopped herself from reaching for his hand. "I've accepted a position as field crew on a fossil dig in Bynum, Montana. Not much money, but it's a start." She exhaled slowly, giving her announcement time to sink in. "I'm leaving on Friday, that's why the suitcases. When I get settled, I'll tell you where to send the boxes."

She pulled a manila envelope from a drawer in the end table and handed it to him.

"What's this?"

"The divorce papers."

He set his glass on the coffee table, ignoring the coaster bought years earlier on a tour of Taos Pueblo. He stood with the envelope but didn't open it. "Even if you get your divorce, Lorene, I'll be here in case you want to come back. Married or not, I'll be here. That's what our vows meant to me."

"Oh, Frank. It's time to let go. Let me go, Frank."

* * *

This story first appeared in the After Dinner Conversation—April 2024 issue.

Discussion Questions

1. Who (*if anyone*) is at fault for the divorce? Frank, for becoming settled in his ways and/or not checking in enough with Lorene about her happiness? Lorene, for initiating the divorce and/or failing to better express her needs?

2. Is a marriage, like Frank says, "till death do us part," or is Lorene right to assert herself to try to find happiness? Does she owe Frank the chance to try and fix their marriage? Does she owe him anything?

3. What does Ruby's response to learning about the pending divorce tell you about their marriage? What would it tell you if Ruby had been more upset about it?

4. Is there an understandable difference between a young marriage and an old marriage? Should an old marriage have the same passion as a new marriage, as Lorene expects?

5. What do you think their relationship will look like in five years? Do you think they will be back together? Be friends that still talk and share? Do you think Loraine will live to regret her choice?

* * *

Lies I Tell My Father

J.G. Alderburke

* * *

Content Disclosure: None

* * *

"How's your job at the newspaper?" my father asks me. He is sitting on a couch, a plush throw blanket spread across his legs.

"The newspaper's fine," I lie.

I lie because it is simple. I lie because it is quick. I lie because it is easier than trying to explain to him yet again that though I have worked for twenty-five years, I have never worked at a newspaper.

My father and I stare at each other. I wait for him to launch into a story about his life. He has about six of these stories, or rather, he has thousands of stories, but only six he remembers at any one time. All of them are old, almost ancient. They happened decades ago and I've heard them hundreds of times already.

I sit in one of two swivel chairs across from the couch; a glass table piled with magazines and newspapers squats between us. We're in the living room of the house I grew up in, the same house my parents have lived in for more than forty years.

My father looks bored. He fusses with the blanket tossed across his legs simply to have something to do. I know from experience that talking to him about current events is useless. Neighborhood news, international intrigues, it's all lost on him because he doesn't recognize any of the names or events.

He looks out the large bay window at the bird feeder my mother hung from a tree branch.

"Look at those things; they're there all the time," my father says and points out the window. He points because he cannot find the words to describe what he's watching. It's as if suddenly his mind is like a large dark room and he's floundering around in it with a very dull flashlight. I can tell by his expression there's more he wants to say, so I wait for it.

"Birds!" he blurts out. "They jump on that hanging thing, then grab a few seeds and disappear."

I nod. My father can watch birds for hours.

"Have you seen any other animals in the yard?" I ask.

My father thinks about this as if he hasn't been asked this question dozens of times. He points to the backyard. "There were two huge deer back there. They walked out of the woods and right across our lawn. Then they went down the driveway, crossed the street, and disappeared behind someone's house."

I smile but there is no joy there. Once, there were acres of woods behind my parents' house. Developers slowly seized all of them. There haven't been deer in the backyard for years.

"Where is Kathleen?" my father asks.

This is a relatively new development. Kathleen is his wife and my mother, though he never used that name with his children, especially when we were young. Adult first names were only used with other adults. She was always "your mother" in our conversations, just as he was "your father" when Mom talked about him.

Even when we were well into adulthood the "your mother" and "your father" monikers stuck. But not lately. Now, every week he asks me where Kathleen is. It makes me wonder if he no longer recognizes me as one of his children.

As to where Mom is, she has escaped, at least temporarily. She's out in the car driving nowhere in particular, just getting away from her duties to Dad for a few hours. He is not healthy enough to be on his own so I come by every weekend as a small relief, a kind of living get-out-of-jail-free card, albeit a temporary one.

I picture my mother cruising around town in her sports car, Willie Nelson blaring from the speakers, the canvas top retracted even though it is a bit chilly for that today.

"Where is Kathleen?" my father repeats.

I consider turning on the television. Like watching birds, my father can watch TV for hours and be perfectly content.

"She's out," I say.

He tilts his head and scowls. "What?" he asks.

Maybe he didn't hear me or maybe he just doesn't like my answer; I can't tell which.

"She went out," I repeat.

"Out with who?"

He is stuck now, trapped in one of his verbal loops. It's happened before. He will ask where Mom is again and again until the moment she's home. I've decided this is an insidious way to slowly drive his listeners insane.

"Kathleen was here a minute ago. I don't know where she went."

"She went to church. She had to go to Mass." The lie pops out of my mouth unexpectedly, like a ghost from a closet.

The scowl leaves my father's face. There are many things he can rail against, but not The Church. He leans back on the cushions and settles into the couch. The loop, as if by magic, is broken. He quietly stares out the bay window for a little while, then points at something. "Have you seen the birds jumping around on that thing out there?"

I am saved from answering by the ring of the telephone bolted to a wall in the kitchen. I recognize the number on the caller ID. It's my sister. She lives on the other side of the country and feels guilty for doing so. She calls our parents and mails them things, sometimes things they actually need. Because of the distance, she never visits; she leaves that to me and my brother.

"I thought you'd be there," she says after she hears my voice. "How is Dad?"

I shrug as if she can see me. "The same. His mind seems a little worse, but maybe I'm imagining that."

"Sorry," she says as if she caused his atrophying brain.

I ask about her husband and she asks about my wife, but really all we want to talk about is our parents.

"Mom's out gallivanting?" she asks.

"For the moment."

"What's on Dad's hit parade today?"

"Stories about Fort Bragg and his big war wound."

"Oh God, not the thumb-he-got-caught-in-the-rifle story."

"That's the one."

My sister sighs. "He's so lucky he never saw combat."

I pace across the kitchen. "He was badgering me about where Mom went like he does every week. Today I couldn't take it. The truth just confuses him, so I told him she went to church."

My sister pauses as if thinking of a response. "Then there's your answer," she says. "Tell him anything that calms him down. Or switch subjects, distract him. Whatever it takes."

Suddenly, I had license to lie.

"Shall I put him on?"

I carry the receiver over to the couch. The phone has a comically long cord expressly for this purpose.

"It's Ashley," I say as I hand him the phone. I leave the rest up to my sister. While they talk, I text my wife.

How much bourbon do we have in the house?

This is a kind of ritual for us. At some point, my wife realized what would help smooth some of the edges created by these parental visits was a large craft cocktail, ideally served the moment I stepped into our house. She tracks my phone on her phone and knows the exact moment to start filling the cocktail shaker.

I hear the ding of a text and look at my phone.

Plenty of bourbon. Perhaps a Manhattan tonight?

I text back.

A double please.

Eventually, I hear my father say goodbye several times and I return the receiver to the kitchen. I count backward from ten and when I hit zero, I poke my head out of the kitchen and look at my father. He is staring at the television screen though the TV is not on. I slip out the side door and walk along the back of the house, then around to the driveway. I open and close the door to my car, take a deep breath, then step on the walkway that leads to the house. I knock a few times on the front door and step inside.

"Hi, Dad. How are you?" I ask.

My father looks surprised. I see a mix of recognition and confusion in his eyes.

"Hey, come in," he says. "Come in and sit down."

I do as I am told.

"How's the newspaper?" he asks.

"They're sending me on a trip," I say.

His eyes open wider.

"They're flying me to Italy to write a story."

He sits up a little straighter. "My grandfather was born in Italy."

Of course I know this, but I pretend I do not.

"Where in Italy?" I ask.

My father knits his brow. "I don't remember. Somewhere in the middle. They have a big family." He starts counting siblings on his fingers. "There's Fannie, Gloria, Ida, George, Tootsie...."

"He was born in Rome," I interrupt. "That's where I'm going."

"Ah, Roma," he says wistfully. "I'd like to go there someday."

"You've been there," I tell him.

My father frowns. "No, I haven't."

"I can prove it." I disappear into the study and rummage through the bookshelves. I emerge with a stack of books, photo albums, city guides, and maps that I lug over to the couch. I open a guidebook to Rome and hold it so my father can see the pictures.

"There's the Colosseum and the Forum," I say to jog his memory and give him some identifying landmarks. Then I grab a photo album and thumb through the pages.

"The newspaper's sending me to Rome so I can talk to the Pope."

My father breaks into a smile. "I saw the Pope."

I stop at pictures my father took of Vatican City, color photos of Castel Sant'Angelo, a Bernini fountain, portraits of Swiss Guards. I point to a picture of St. Peter's Square. A small man in white robes is standing on a balcony.

"Who's that?" I ask.

My father leans closer to the picture. "That's the Pope." He smiles and takes the album from me. "Look at all the people there." He touches the picture as if to make sure it is real, then shifts his gaze to other photographs on the page. He points to a picture of two people standing in front of an ornate fountain.

"That's me, and that's your mother," he tells me as if I would not recognize them.

I let him look through several pages, then distract him with a map of Italy.

"Here's Rome," I say as I point to a section of the map. "You also went to Siena one year. Up here." I drag my finger to another section of the map. "You went to the Palio with Roger."

My father looks unconvinced. "Who's Roger?"

"Your other son," I explain, then open another album. "You went to watch the horse races." I point to a picture of horses running in circles.

My father looks at the picture, initially with a blank

expression, then it's as if a switch goes on in his head. "They build a track in the middle of the town and everyone jams in around it. People are screaming and cheering and placing bets. Then, the horses fly around the track. It's wild." His eyes fix on mine. "Have you been there?"

"You went with Roger," I repeat. "Your son Roger. He ran track in high school, remember? He did the hurdles."

I scramble through a photo book until I find a picture my father took. It shows Roger mid-flight over a hurdle, a study in energy and grace. Roger looks like he's gliding over the hurdle, one leg forward, one back, arms outstretched; every part of his body streamlined except one: his hair. It sticks up and out at odd angles, blown in all directions by the wind.

"He was fast," my father says as he looks at the picture. "He blew by everybody on the track he was so good. He was always running. I bet he's still running."

"Yeah, he is," I say though I know my brother developed arthritis in one knee and had replacement surgery a month ago. "He won a few medals last weekend."

My father gasps. He pulls the blanket off his legs and hands me the photo album. "I want to show you something." He stands and wobbles into the dining room past a row of framed photographs on the wall and stops in front of a series of tall, narrow frames. Each one has a circular gold or silver medal attached to a long red-and-blue ribbon.

"These are some of Roger's medals. Have you seen them?"

I shake my head no, allowing my body to lie for me.

"I'm telling you, Roger is very good."

I point to a picture in the photo album I'm holding. "That's Roger, and that's you in front of a Greek restaurant in

Siena. You jokers fly all the way to Italy and eat in probably the only Greek restaurant in the country."

My father laughs a hearty, booming laugh I remember from childhood. "It was a good restaurant," he says.

I wake up the smart speaker on the dining room table and tell it to play sirtaki dance music. A mandolin and bouzouki begin to play, the rhythm slow and steady at first, then building hypnotically to something faster and irresistible. My father arcs his arms in the air then swings them back and forth in a bad imitation of Zorba the Greek. I am afraid he will hurt himself or fall over. I divert his attention to the photographs on the wall.

"Tell me where those are," I say.

My father uses his cane to point to a giant chasm carved into the earth. "That's the Grand Canyon," he tells me. "I rode a donkey on a trail all the way to the bottom. At the bottom, there was a lake and we all went swimming. The water was freezing."

There are parts of this story I have never heard before and I make a mental note to confirm how much of it is true.

My father points to a hill bathed in the golden glow of sunset. "That's a mountain somewhere in the Grand Canyon. We went on tours to look for cave drawings and dinosaur bones."

He uses his cane to totter back to the couch and sits down. "What happened to the music?"

The Greek tune plays again. This time my father waves his arms and snaps his fingers as he sits on the couch.

"Louder," he yells.

Like the wheels of a train the pace of the music gathers steam; the rhythm teases and entices like a seduction; the notes fly together creating an urgency, a need to move, and suddenly even I start shuffling my feet and twirling my arms. I command the music to play louder, and my father and I move as if spellbound, powerless, like puppets whose limbs are controlled by the strings of a mandolin. A spell broken only when my mother bursts through the front door.

"Looks like you two are having fun."

I lower the music. "I can't really explain this," I say.

"No need to." She puts down her packages and joins my father on the couch. "What are you looking at?"

I gather the bags that have groceries and head for the kitchen. I pour glasses of lemonade, assemble a tray of Italian cookies, and carry them to the living room.

"You've heard a lot of stories, I'm guessing," my mother says.

"A few I haven't heard for a while," I reply.

We talk until I decide it's time to go. My mother hugs me goodbye; my father and I shake hands.

When I am in my car, I text my wife.

Just leaving my parents' house now.

I hear the ding of an incoming text.

I'm tracking your route. I'll have the Manhattan waiting.

That's right, the drink. I had preordered alcohol like you do at the opera or Broadway shows. It's hard for me to believe but I'd forgotten about it, perhaps didn't even need it. The edge I usually feel after these visits isn't there. I put the car into reverse and back out of the driveway. I could text my wife and save her the trouble of concocting cocktails. I could, but I do not. Instead, I drive home. Who am I to give up the distinct pleasures of a handcrafted double Manhattan?

* * *

This story first appeared in the After Dinner Conversation—February 2024 issue.

Discussion Questions

1. How important is it for the narrator to tell his father the truth? Should he simply agree with whatever incorrect assertions the father makes about their lives?

2. Was the narrator wrong to leave the house, then knock on the door and pretend to enter for the first time? What is acceptable and unacceptable deceit, and how do you know which is which?

3. When her father no longer recognizes the son, does the narrator still have an obligation to come visit or to simply pay a caretaker to watch over his father so his mother can get out of the house?

4. At what point of memory loss (*if any*) should the father be allowed to die, even if his body is otherwise in good condition?

5. What would you do if you realized you were getting dementia and would, in a few years, no longer remember family members?

* * *

Q-tip Options

Steve Parker

* * *

<u>Content Disclosure</u>: Substance Addiction Themes; Strong Language

* * *

1 – A week before I thought I should write this down

I am not a good person. Abby was at my door. My reaction when I saw her should have been more charitable. She was young and cute and needy, but all I wanted was a nice relaxing day at home. When the police questioned her, I should have let them take her away. Jail would have been tough, but it would have been better for her than coming to me. Now she was here, and I will always regret what I would do with the Q-tips.

It was unexpected when she rang the doorbell, the pretentious Big Ben sounding "bong" in that small foyer. Never invited to visit, but, still, here she stood on my doorstep. From the Walmart sign where Abby spent her days, my house was visible. It was one of those hot and humid Georgia days reflected on her face. She was flushed and feverish looking. Something was wrong.

"I need a shower." Not a flirtatious schtick, it was the tone of someone at the check-in desk of a hospital. Robert was in jail. At times, he would sit on the rock with her at the Walmart sign, but now he was gone, and she was living alone in their tent in the weeds.

"Are you okay?" And with that, like I always do, I invited another complication into my life.

* * *

2 – Three months before I thought I should write this down

Abby's spot by the Walmart sign was her place of business, her and Robert's. Ride a loop through the neighborhood on a bicycle, and most mornings, she'd be there on what became her corner. That's how we met. I never regretted the conversations we had; after my estranged daughter and my ex-wife left, I enjoyed those little chats. It wasn't love. It was a time machine. An old man instinctively talking to a young woman.

Of course, some conversations are driven by desperation and calculation. We all do something like that according to our circumstances. Every conversation has at least two charted courses—one person has a direction, simple or complicated, and the other person has something different. Maybe you want to affirm a friendship with a gentle exchange of trivial nothings, or maybe you need money for drugs. None of it is ever the whole story. When Abby paid attention, she was a surprisingly good listener who was smart but not cunning the way one would expect from a person living on the side of the road. Sometimes her brain would be somewhere else, but when she was there, she was smart, funny, and bewildering.

Morning, 8:30 a.m. Abby was out with her sign. Strange, they would have such early hours. Early mornings always seemed connected to hardworking people.

"Sleeping all day used to be the only thing I ever wanted to do when I was your age. Now that I can, I'm not capable of it."

"What? Why?"

"I'm retired. I can sleep all I want, but I can't sleep. Four hours usually, five on a good night."

"I don't like to sleep. It's not good for you."

"No, I don't think that's right."

Silence, and a shrug, then, "Maybe. I don't know. It's probably different for you. You know, old people." She looked at me. "I'm sorry." She could have regretted what she said, or she could have felt she was losing her negotiating position. She turned away for a moment. "But you're okay, aren't you? Do you do anything? Something to help?"

What the hell did that mean? Then chuckling. "Ice cream. It doesn't help, but any excuse for ice cream is a good thing."

* * *

3 – Customers - Same Day

Historically, what they were doing was the way people have always started up enterprises. Pick a spot, put up a sign. Strangers are even better in some ways than friends to talk to. You don't owe them anything after you finish a conversation. And Abby, she was open to questions. She liked the break in her routine. Who could blame her?

Abby and Robert lived on convenience store junk. I would feel like a hero if I showed up with anything bordering on healthy, like a boxed salad to go with the not-so-healthy

Mountain Dew and the Twizzlers she liked. She jumped at my offer to pick something up for her. "Twizzlers!" she quickly said. Her instant request for Twizzlers became confusing because there were so many varieties.

"Strawberry. Oh God, not the licorice. And not the grape or cherry or watermelon ones. Somebody said they had a chocolate kind once. No. No, thank you. I used to like the cherry cola and the rainbow kinds. Not now. Strawberry. And not the Pull and Peel ones, just the regular, eight-inch Twizzlers."

It is important to know what you want in life.

"You want to come and pick them out?"

Shrug, meaning yes.

"Thank you. I can't sort through all of that."

When we entered the store, she swooped down without breaking stride and scooped up a red marker lost on the floor. She patted the pen in her pocket like a trophy. I would learn how much she liked to draw. Something changed in her when she drew and decorated new signs. She kept her pens and markers wrapped in some papers.

Abby's daily forty-dollar target was for oxycodone, she told me. A friend of mine insisted it was for heroin, but why did that even matter? It's poison, no matter how many ways culture sells it. Poison somehow delivered with the lure of easy money, or easy something, because there must have been a point when she thought she was doing something leading to, what, happiness? Before she simply had to do things to get by.

"I was an early adopter."

She put her sign down. "Well, that's good, whatever that is. What are you talking about?"

"Dope, drugs. Not like this, though."

"I thought we were done with that."

"We are. I mean, I'm talking about me. I mean, you do what you want. I just don't want to sound like I am some kind of good guy."

Her eyebrow twitched. "I don't like it when somebody thinks they're better than me."

"No. That's exactly not what I'm saying." Scratching my teeth with my lip, I continued. "I'm not better than anybody. Back when, this stuff was tame. A little pot. Get a little silly. Maybe a doctor's prescription for something. To be honest, this shit scares me. I don't like being out of control."

Another forty dollars was for Robert. Their daily goal, and it's funny that people helped them get there. All those people knew was something sad on the side of the road. Deep down at their very cores, people in this world are built around tiny original nougats of goodness. It's born there, and the layers are all added after that first neonatal moment when we enter this world. The ugly stuff gets wrapped on later. Food and dollar bills from well-meaning people came out of car windows for them. Always given to Abby. Robert stayed out of sight or a short distance to the side because the car windows were more generous to Abby.

Their cardboard sign read "living on a prayer." Sometimes they would change the wording to "living on Jesus" or "anything helps." Abby would lose herself when she used the pens and markers to change their sign.

"You having fun?"

"Uh-huh."

"I like the way you make the letters three-dimensional looking."

"Uh-huh."

"The colors are nice. Did someone teach you how to match up complementary colors like that?"

"Nope."

"Do you like doing that, drawing?"

"Uh-huh"

This was a twenty-five-year-old child; she went to a pleasant place while she drew. It was rude of me to try to talk to her there, to bring her back here. What happened to the little girl in grade school drawing crayon landscapes? Does she still exist somewhere? Uh-huh. Albert Einstein demonstrated to the world that the concept of time is a physical thing. The past is not just a memory; it is a thing that still exists in a place we can't see or get to or interact with. Somewhere, third-grade Abby is still struggling to master colored pencils. Uh-huh.

* * *

4 – Pillows - two months before I thought I should write this down

When Abby and Robert hit their combined eighty-dollar goal, they were done for the day. Their income wasn't bad for the hours invested. If the drugs weren't killing them and draining the purpose from them, it wouldn't be such a bad way to make a living. Their lives were centered there on that corner and in that tent where they slept. What were their mornings like? I had seen Robert before, in the early morning, walking to the gas station and returning with two coffees. Terrible coffee at that place. They loved anything with caffeine in it. And what did they talk about during quiet hours across pillows? I wondered. They had pillows. I saw them, blue, not too dark, and clean.

"Those look comfortable."

A soft pat on one. "Yes." She smoothed a spot of the fabric.

They must have told themselves some version of life to shape their world, organized along an axis. We all do that. Our minds are, after all, like relentless little organic Roombas, constantly in motion, vacuuming up the dust and lint of our thoughts. Did they share those thoughts with each other at night, plan a future, talk about the next day? To make their tomorrows into workable concepts, their visions and dreams would certainly be archaic and convoluted. They took comfort from each other. You could tell that by watching them interact. They shared the belief that each knew and understood the other. But ultimately, isn't thinking about what other people are thinking the most destructive thing we do and seldom accurate? Or does that only apply when we think we know what strangers are thinking? Divorce statistics argue against that.

* * *

5 – Two months before I thought I should write this down

Ken Kesey's Chief had a bottle that drank the person. But drugs, they devour everything. Locusts inside the soul. I didn't know much about Abby's supply chain. She only told me about the character she bought her drugs from. Nature documentaries tell us about him: a parasitic creature living off another organism and harming the host. It's not even a symbiotic relationship where both benefit from the relationship.

She was certain she was doing the only thing she could do, following her only available options.

"We're doing the best we can," she had once told me.

"Have you ever thought about rehab?"

They were polite. They had this conversation before.

They feigned interest and played off one another to move the conversation along to a different place.

* * *

6 – One and a half months before

Abby tried to frame it as a job.

"I have to go to work now."

I laughed. "Will you get fired?"

"It's panhandling."

"What is the difference between panhandling and begging?"

Spinning the sign between her fingers, "It's what I do."

"And what, no retirement benefits?"

"And a 401K."

We tried a small laugh, but it didn't get off the ground. The words were forced. Me with nothing to add, her slow to go back to the roadside. I imagined her working in an evil cartoon factory, whistles blowing somewhere in the background. She grabbed her cardboard and started her workday.

* * *

7 – Hosing down the driveway - one month before writing this down

I was hosing down my driveway, making little lines of the leaves and debris, then pushing them backward in uniform ranks. There, just at the corner of the house on the edge of the driveway, through a small break in the foliage where it was possible to see Abby's spot, two police cruisers. Robert was in the back seat of one. I turned off the water.

There are significant levels of violence in that part of Decatur, right at the edge of Atlanta's Zone 5, so vagrants are not usually an urgent issue. Invariably, however, someone will complain. Tolerated up to a point, then, well, something gets done. Robert had been carted off by the time I got there.

The remaining officer stepped closer to Abby. He had that police voice of technical politeness with the undertone of threat. "I explained it; you can't do that here."

She nodded, holding her sign behind her. She played this game. Whenever a police car drove by, she would throw her sign out of sight. She thought that protected her. Made her innocent. If you can't see me holding a sign in my hand, I'm not here doing this.

All I had planned was a nice relaxing day at home.

"We talked about rehab, Officer."

He looked at me, then back to Abby. She remained silent. She wanted to be outside of the conversation, to be informed about the outcome.

"I live right there." I pointed, but he waved me off and concentrated on her.

Backing off and forming his decision, "You just can't stand around here with that sign. Okay?"

Still not talking, she nodded her head. She was on notice. Next time he would take her too.

I hadn't lied. It wasn't entirely untrue, but it was misleading. She already nixed the rehab idea. He left her with a number to call. They'd tell her how to get Robert bailed out. He walked back to his cruiser. Underneath it all, she cared for Robert. One more sadness.

* * *

8 – Mausoleum - Thursday

Two miles away is the site of the world's very first Waffle House. I am disproportionately proud of that. Across the city lines, Atlanta is the home of Coca-Cola. The Greater Metropolitan Atlanta has absorbed everything around it, though not everyone agrees that is a good thing. Decatur is a separate city. Together they're famous to the rest of the world for greasy food and sugary beverages.

All I wanted was a nice relaxing evening at home. I was driving in across the British bridges. At Jimmy Carter Boulevard, a strange traffic configuration crosses Interstate 85. All the lanes switch over to opposite sides on the bridge so that the oncoming traffic is to the right, only for crossing the bridge. For a moment, the traffic is British. I don't understand how it makes the traffic flow better. It does, but part of me still feels like it is wrong for traffic to pass by on the "wrong" side. A small panicky feeling always rides with me at that point. I keep wondering about London. Would a bridge routing traffic over to the right side, their "other side," would that solve a traffic problem there? I can't doublethink through the layers.

It was late in the day. I don't believe in omens—at least, I say that. Sometimes I let strange things make my decisions and determine my explanations for me. If one outcome happens, then it will settle some other undecided thing for me. One potato, two potato, after all, is a rigged system. Turning off from six-lane Memorial onto two-lane Midway, eight turning vehicles waited in front of me. Eight blinking turn signals. An uncomfortable and eerie feeling came over me. Something was about to happen. The blinking lights in front of me were organizing, as if they were trying to synchronize, blink, blink... blink. And then they did exactly that. They all blinked together, one time only. BLINK! A one-act chorus just for me. I looked behind me. Something, I didn't know what, felt wrong. I wanted to tell someone. The turn signals once again became chaotic. With an ethereal sense of the moment that felt like an intuition, I flipped off my blinker and jumped lanes. I had not checked on Abby for a while.

They were gone. No surprise. I don't know what I expected. The walk up to the tent site distorted my sense of proprioception, the way you know you are moving in an elevator. The sensation was augmented by faint crunching sounds underfoot and the overall feeling that it is never fully daylight here, nor is it ever completely night.

I saw the problem around the tent. Everything they owned was scattered, deserted, or discarded outside of the tattered nylon shelter. I tried to tell myself that Robert had come back, and they simply moved on. But things they would have taken were abandoned in front of me. The pillows were here. Abby had a funny way of talking about going home in the evenings. Maybe she didn't want to talk about going to a tent; she would say she wanted to put her head on her pillow. That always hurt me to think about being exhausted, wanting to go home for a nap and trying to hide the fact that home is a tent. I saw the pillows were still here. She would have taken them— probably. Her precious markers and folded paper, however, were even more disconcerting. They were like the chalk outline left behind by a forensic team.

The twilight shadows of the mausoleum behind me crawled up the hill and crept up my back. The air cooled the way it does around here in the evenings. Abby was gone. It should not have affected me. They would build a Covid testing center over this parking lot, but that too would soon be gone. Things change, usually without explanation. Everything around here goes somewhere else.

* * *

9 – Q-tips - A week before I thought I should write this down

The shower helped. It revived her. The effects of the heat and the grime of the streets had been diminished. She asked for a Q-tip, and to this day, I am punished by the thoughtlessness of my response. Her face had brightened when she saw the little, unopened travel-size box of cotton swabs. It was an image of something made for travel that gripped her, not the Q-tips. It was such a small thing, and the situation went unrecognized by me. "Take some from the big, open box." I was a thoughtless host. It wasn't the cotton swabs; it was the concept. The travel-size box was a thing designed so it could travel with her, like a form of furniture for her portable existence. It was a thing created for an unanchored life. The lack of recognition I exhibited of her simple desire to have that inconsequential thing still bothers me and always will. A small thing, maybe, but always a regret.

That was not the point at which Abby was going to change and rebuild her life. As soon as the clean water had showered away the heat and relieved some of the deadweight of the way she was living, a measure of vitality flowed back into her, and she began orchestrating her exit. Needs that had taken her dreams called out to her like a key turned in an ignition. Vulnerable, and nothing I could do would help her. Not really. That was the last time I saw her. The little tent in the weeds remained for a time.

* * *

10 – Mausoleum background - last Thursday

She liked to draw. She had cried when I asked her what her life would be like in two years. I looked at the sketches folded around her little bundle of pens and markers. The conversation we had about drawing would later dart past my head like a bat in the twilight, something glimpsed and too evasive to grab and hold.

I never asked why she and Robert chose to homestead in that specific stand of trees between the forsaken remains of Columbia Mall parking lots below and the active Walmart lots above. Columbia Mall died and disappeared when the white citizens moved on, and finally, none other than Chuck Norris blew the buildings up in 1985 to make the movie *Invasion USA*.

Walmart came but was not interested in the now neglected and overgrown lower parking lots. No one cared what happened there. Everything down there wasted away, abandoned. A small regret remains that I didn't know the backstory of the mall and of the mausoleum. I could have told Abby and Robert about the history of the place. Descendants of George Washington's brother Samuel are buried there. I had been a poor tour guide.

One thing that remained after Columbia Mall faded was that mausoleum. Architects designing the Columbia Mall had decided to grade down fifteen feet around the Cawley family cemetery, thus converting it into a raised Mausoleum. Local wits call it the Tomb of the Unknown Shopper. Facing the tent site was that tall, square, stone fortress of a mausoleum with a Dracula-style iron gate leading into the base, up an interior stairway to the top. When Abby and Robert were gone, I would wonder if that iron gate had been dragged open. I should have inspected it.

When night approaches the mausoleum grows, the shadows crawl up the hill. The overgrown brush-shades come along in step, but the mausoleum rises highest, advances fastest, vectors in on the tent. It resembles the looming square shoulders of some monstrous thing moving through the twilight.

The name of that area is Belvedere Park, no city or government functions. The name is simply to distinguish it from the places it isn't, Decatur and Atlanta. The word *belvedere* comes from two Italian words which mean good view. Odd. View of what? Night here is never the night we have elsewhere. It is never completely dark with the sodium arc lights on the streets. It wasn't the change of light and dark that chilled the heart, never bright, in perpetual eclipse. The light is better out on the street, and the dark is darker on the edge of the woods, darker yet farther back in the woods. Midway between Atlanta and Decatur, midway between Walmart and the road named Midway, this is a place in the margins. Things good and bad happen in the margins.

The two-hundred-year-old cemetery is now a mausoleum, smaller than a hotel but larger than a campsite. Family member plots were marked with headstones, but scattered around had been unmarked graves of slaves and poor whites. Construction grading of the surrounding area leveled out parking lots for Columbia Mall. That's still a controversial decision. Fifteen feet above the surroundings, the mausoleum remains. The unmarked burial sites are gone. Abby and Robert are gone as if the mausoleum consumed them all. The abandoned lower lots are a maze of paved surfaces outlined by brush and saplings, shadows and sounds. At times, the incongruous beat of a nearby Charter Arts school marching band drifts down to the lower lots and the mausoleum.

* * *

11 – The tent - still Thursday

I picked up Abby's parcel of pens and the folded papers. An unspecified sense of loss stirred in me. This should have been with her, not here. I was invading her special locus by looking at it. It was her private place where she conjured a little brightness. I ignored the eclectic collection of colored pencils, pens, and markers. Those were only the tools. The several sheets of unsophisticated artwork were something more significant. The drawings were confidential hieroglyphics closeted in an intimate language to herself for esoteric purposes. Puerile at first glance, her drawings were free of culture's constraints. These were like stick figures, but somehow an artistic quality was in them. The sense of the images formed an order of sorts, but I would not know the story they told.

The figures were unfamiliar poses, like ancient cultures, drawn in a style of their own. And houses. Houses showing families, looking like assignments from child psychologists, mother, father, and child drawn in odd proportions. She had an undeveloped talent. Lots of drawings of furniture and floor plans. Fancy dresses. No food but two babies. And a beach scene. Larger than the other images, an iPhone. When she came to my house, even before her shower and the Q-tips, when she was still feeling bumpy and sick, the first thing she did after walking in the door was to charge her crappy little battered phone, struggling with the connections. It was her contact with the larger world. These pictures were clues in an unknown language, pointing toward a direction I could not see.

I should have simply let the police officer take her away. There could have been the possibility of some sort of redemption. At least I could think she might still be alive.

* * *

12 – Ziplocks – since the Q-tips incident

The city, or Walmart, or maybe a landowner clear-cut the lot. Even the vacant tent is gone. In the back seat of my car, I keep little ziplock bags I call goodie bags. Tributes, perhaps, to the guilt of knowing I'm not a good person, and probably anger inspired by guilt is what drives it more than altruistic motives. It upsets me when I see someone panhandling on the side of the road, not from contempt, but because I know I will feel guilty if I ignore them. If I give them money, I know I am supporting a drug problem. The only thing I came up with was food or these little ziplock bags. Not philanthropy, a defense. They are filled with hygiene products and small treats, little bags of trail mix or dried fruit, along with a folded paper in each with contact information for homeless shelters and helplines. It's not a new thing. I had goodie bags in my car before I met Abby, but now the treats are a little better quality, and they have little travel-size boxes of Q-tips.

* * *

13 – Today

Donna lives in her battered Honda Odyssey in the corner of a large Walmart parking lot. A different Walmart.

"Donna, how are you doing?"

She nods as she sorts through boxes and small broken bicycles surrounding her Honda.

"It's hot today. I'm going inside. You want some water,

maybe lemonade?"

"No, I drink tea and (something inaudible). Cold tea. I got some."

"I left some things tied to your door handle the day before yesterday. Did you find them?"

Nods and again something inaudible. I don't blame her. Life is embarrassing.

"I can get you one of those salads."

"No. No thanks." Sometimes she gets maybe confused, maybe suspicious of who knows what, and these days who can blame her? Sixty to look at her, probably more like fifty but with mileage. Movies depict homeless people as if they are normal people under sad circumstances. As if conversations would sound like neighbors talking over a fence. It's not like that. It's rude to talk about mental illness, but they live in fear and desperation. Watch your fingers aren't bitten.

"How about another bag with the little soaps and shampoo and stuff?"

She smiles.

The bag has Q-tips.

* * *

This story first appeared in the After Dinner Conversation—October 2023 issue.

Discussion Questions

1. Why do you think the narrator has such an interest in Abby and in homeless people in general? Is the narrator motivated by altruism, curiosity, or something else?
2. Do you think the narrator is doing the right thing by talking to Abby and Robert? Is he genuinely interacting with Abby, or being manipulated as a resource by a culture he is not a participant in?
3. Should the narrator put conditions on the support given to Abby (*you must enter rehab*), or should humane actions come without conditions? Is the narrator enabling Abby's addiction by helping her without conditions?
4. Does Abby even need help? Or do individuals have an inherent right to make their own choices, including the choice to live on the street and take drugs every day?
5. Should the narrator have let the police arrest Abby? What do you think would have happened next?

* * *

Visions of Midwives

C.S. Griffel

* * *

<u>Content Disclosure</u>: Medical Procedures; Mild Violence

* * *

The heavy groan sounded as though it were being dragged from inside the woman's body involuntarily. Her pregnant belly heaved as guttural sounds enveloped the tiny bedroom. Keery dabbed the sweat from the woman's forehead. The midwife, Luanne, examined the woman to check her dilation. A clock on the mantelpiece ticked away the minutes, piling them into hours.

"Illona, you're doing so well, darling. Your baby's head has engaged, and you're going to really start pushing."

Illona responded with only a nod and "uh-huh."

"Keery, come here, girl," Luanne ordered. Keery obeyed quickly. "Place your hand here. Feel that? That's how you can tell the baby's head is engaged. Illona, on your next contraction, you're going to push." Keery was nearing the end of her apprenticeship, so it was not the first time she had felt a baby's head engaged. Still, she obeyed. Each experience was building Keery up, readying her for her practice.

The process went quickly. It was Illona's sixth baby. Within a few pushes, the baby's head was completely born.

"One more big push, Illona, and your baby will be born." Illona's contraction hit; she scrunched her face until it looked like a closed fist and pushed. Luanne's hands grabbed ahold of the baby as he was suspended in the space between being born and not yet born. The elderly midwife's eyes rolled back as a vision of the child's destiny encompassed her mind. The moment was over as quickly as it had come. The little boy was born. For the briefest moment, Keery saw that Luanne's features were grim. Before Illona could see her face, she wiped it clean of emotion.

"Is it a boy?" Illona asked, her voice breathy and rough from the effort of getting her child out into the world.

"Yes, it's a boy," was Luanne's dry reply.

Keery looked at the tiny baby. He looked perfect. He balled his little hands into fists and kicked with both his legs. She wondered what Luanne had seen. Keery had not yet experienced the second sight, but she knew she would when her turn came to be the attending midwife.

"Take care of Illona, Keery, while I take care of the mite."

Keery's job now was to wait for Illona's body to complete the process of birth. Soon the placenta would appear. Illona did not know that Luanne had seen her son's future. It was a secret long kept by the midwives of their people. The clock tower in the town square chimed out a quarter past one in the morning.

Keery noted that the little boy had not yet cried. Illona noticed too.

"Is he all right?" Illona's voice, roughened from groaning, broke the quiet. Luanne did not respond immediately. "Midwife, is he all right, I say?" At this, Luanne wrapped the boy in the soft blanket his mother had carefully knitted for him. Illona didn't have much in the way of wealth, but each of her babies at least got a new blanket, even if it was knitted from yarn carefully undone from his dad and grandad's old sweaters.

Luanne brought the little man to his mother, only his face visible in the mass of soft yarn, just yellow enough to not be white. The midwife handed the waiting mother her child. The mother's eyes were full of fear and love. She glanced at her baby's face, his closed eyes.

"He never drew the first breath of life," Luanne delivered the words gently, but they struck the mother like a fist to her gut. The woman gathered her baby to her, and a wail like the cold winter wind barreling through the high mountains grew out of the woman's belly and shattered the peaceful calm of deep night.

Keery wondered what had happened. She had seen the boy born. He had been kicking and balling up his tiny fists. She knew he had been alive. Confused, Keery glanced at the senior midwife. Luanne's face was a mask of stoic resolve. It was not the time or place to ask questions.

Upon hearing her mournful wail, Illona's husband rushed into the room. He climbed into the bed with his distraught wife and drew her and the baby to himself. He murmured into her ear that he loved her, would always love her, but he did not tell her to be quiet or that it would be okay. He simply allowed her to pour out her grief. Uncaring that they had an audience, the husband held his distraught wife, lest the pain take her away with her child.

Keery helped Luanne gather their things quickly. It was best at this point to leave the grieving family to their pain. It would be the father's job to care for the wee body now. Before they left, the father said, "Your payment is on the mantel, good wife." It was ill luck, even under the circumstances, to leave the midwife unpaid.

As they walked through the damp cold of the night, Keery struggled to put her question into words. What had happened to the child? She alone knew that the midwife had lied. That baby was alive when it was born.

"Luanne..." Keery began. Luanne anticipated the question.

"Child, you will understand when you birth your first baby. You will know when you see what the future has in store. That child was destined for great misery. 'Twas a mercy I done. It is a burden we midwives carry, the purpose of our gift." Her words were sharp and final. Keery knew she would answer no more questions. They parted company near the town square, Luanne to her snug, well-appointed home, Keery to the hovel where she still lived with her parents.

Keery did not sleep that night. She kept thinking of the tiny, perfect arms and legs, unused to the immense space outside the womb, making small, jerking movements, feeling for the boundaries of its new life.

The waning summer brought with it many births. The cold nights of December—all the harvest work done and winter settling in—brought with it many conceptions. Husbands, no longer exhausted from the hard labor of spring, summer, and fall, more frequently sought the affections of their wives.

August was the midwives' busiest month. It also brought an end to Keery's apprenticeship. "There are too many babies coming for me to hold yer hand any longer," Luanna told her as July closed. "We'll place you with the younger mothers who've already had a babe or two." These tended to be the easiest births. The mothers were young enough that the risk of complication was low but had already proven their ability to birth healthy babies.

Keery was summoned for her first birth on August 5 at one in the morning. It was, of course, a full moon. Luanne's errand girl, Peony, rapped loudly on the door, waking Keery and her parents. Keery would not be able to move into her own home until she had earned enough from attending births to purchase one. Her vocation as midwife meant that she would never have a husband. She did not mourn this fact. She had seen many women, married in the rush of youth's lusts, walk an unhappy path when passions cooled. She had also seen young couples wed soberly and advisedly and remain in love their whole lives. Her chances, she supposed, were as good as any to go either way. She simply knew that it was not her destiny to wed. It was part of the midwife's second sight.

"Mildred Connor has gone into labor and needs attendance," Peony said urgently. "Mistress Luanne is attending Morgrid's birth and cannot leave. It's not going well. She sent me to fetch you. She says you must attend Mildred on your own."

Keery nodded and grabbed her midwifery satchel. It had been a gift from the Midwives' Guild and still smelled and creaked like brand-new leather. "Tell Mistress Luanne I'm on my way." Peony scurried quickly into the darkness.

The walk to the Connors' home was about twenty minutes. Mildred's husband answered the door with a look of relief on his face. "It's going quickly," he said. Keery nodded in response and followed him to the back room where Mildred lay upon the bed, knees tucked back as far as they would go, sweat dripping gently down her forehead. As Keery walked in, Mildred was gripped with a contraction that made her push with all her might. Before Keery could reach her, Mildred's body reflexively pushed out a baby girl. Keery moved to check the baby was all right while Mildred took deep breaths, an automatic response to normalize her breathing. When Keery's hands touched the baby, she received no second sight. This child's destiny remained in the realm of the unknown and the unknowable. It happened often enough that a baby was born before a midwife could arrive, especially with healthy babies. It is only in the moment when the child is suspended between being born and not yet born, when the head has emerged, that midwives receive the sight. Frankly, Keery was relieved. The burden of knowing another person's destiny was frightening, and she was glad to put it off, if even for one more day.

Keery checked over the baby, who showed every sign of being quite healthy. After cleaning the baby, Keery handed her over to her mother, who cooed over her beautiful child in the way just birthed mothers do. "Hello, my darling," she purred into the child's ear, "aren't you pretty?" Mildred rained kisses upon the head of fine, raven black hair. Keery waited with Mildred until her placenta was born, checking that all was well. When mother, child, and happy family were well settled, she slipped into the bright midday sun, pleased with herself.

Coins jingled merrily in Keery's little purse as she strode through the village on her way home. It wasn't until Peony crossed her path that she noted the somber air of the village. "Peony," she called, "how is Morgrid? Did her child fare well?" Morgrid and her husband had been childless for the first twenty-three years of their marriage. The couple had long since given up hope of ever having a child when Morgrid found she was finally pregnant at forty-two.

The child looked up at Keery, shaking her head, "No," she said. "Morgrid and her babe died."

It was common for there to be complications in birth for first-time mothers in their thirties or forties. Keery was saddened but not shocked at the outcome. This, too, was a part of midwifery, dealing with the loss of mothers in birth. The midwives did all they could to shepherd mother and baby safely through the process, but sometimes, there was nothing they could do. Death was fated.

It was three weeks later when Keery was summoned once again to attend the birth of a young, fourth-time mother. When Keery arrived, the woman's husband answered the door, drunk. "She's in there," the man said as he pointed to a room on the west side of the house, his stance unsteady. Three young children huddled together in a corner. The eldest sister, no more than eight, sat in between two little boys, looking to be about five and three years old, respectively. The sister's arms were protectively draped over the shoulders of her little brothers. She had a hardened look in her eye, something sad to see in one so young. The little girl made eye contact with Keery, and a little smile crossed the child's lips, a welcome for the young midwife. A groan came from the westward room, and the child's eyes darted back to her father as he shouted, "Quit yer yowlin'! It's giving me a headache!" Hardness replaced the brief smile in the child's eyes.

"Why don't you step outside, sir, where your wife's cries won't bother you. She'll be fine now that I'm here. It looks like your girl there can look well after her brothers." The man nodded, stumbled out the door, and headed for the pub, Keery was sure. He looked like he had once been handsome, but drink and misery had twisted him into an ugly facsimile of his younger self.

The woman in the bed clung to the headboard rails like a drowning person might cling to driftwood in a raging river. Unlike her husband, prettiness still lingered on this woman's face. Love for her children kept her from total despair.

"You're Agnes, aren't you?" Keery inquired. The woman nodded in reply. "I'm Keery, the midwife. I want you to take some deep breaths." Agnes obeyed and breathed in deeply through her nose. Predictably, Agnes's labor went quickly. She seemed to relax with her husband gone and a midwife present.

No more than thirty minutes after Keery's arrival, the baby's head emerged from the birth canal. Keery placed her hands on the tiny head to support the child as its mother completed the birthing process. When the vision overtook her, the pain was so intense Keery thought she would explode into dust, down to the very last molecule. The sensation lasted only a moment, but within it, Keery felt what seemed an eternity pass. She knew now what Luanne had told her about. She knew this child would experience intense suffering. Yet, as she looked at the tiny, beautiful little girl, now fully born, she knew she could not do what Luanne had done. Keery didn't know if this meant she was cowardly or courageous. She only knew she could not extinguish the light of life burning in the milky blue eyes now blinking up at her.

Keery handed the child to her mother. "A lovely little girl," she said. And like all mothers, Agnes drew the child to herself, murmuring and cooing.

"Margery," Keery heard Agnes whisper. Whatever else may come in this child's life, she was loved and content in this moment with this mother.

Misery did come to the child. When Margery was just three years old, Agnes came to a sad end. A merchant in the marketplace allowed his eyes to linger upon her too long. Her husband, in a drunken and jealous rage, beat her to death, and he was hung the next morning, leaving their four children orphans. No one could afford to take in four children, and they were all separated. Within a few months, the families that had taken in the children woke to find their beds empty. The eldest sister had come in the night for her siblings, unwilling to be apart. What became of them after that, no one in the village knew. Keery surmised the child had gone to the city and taken up prostitution to keep her siblings under a roof and fed. There was appetite enough in the big city, even for very young girls, to keep body and soul together for the little orphans. Keery wondered if she was wrong not to have released Margery from this fate.

Most of Keery's visions portended a mixture of pain, sorrow, joy, and peace. All human lives have some of everything. Of course, there were lives that held more or less joy, more or less pain than others, but she had not yet again felt the pain that had been foretold for Margery. Keery, carefully saving every coin, now lived in a small cottage of her own. It was not ostentatious. In fact, it was small and lacked any luxury, but it was tidy and her own. Keery was now a well-loved midwife, popular with young mothers.

Keery awoke naturally in her own bed for the first time in three days. She had just overseen a first-time mother, and the labor had been slow. Even so, baby was well born, and mother was resting in the glow of new motherhood and the love of a proud husband. She looked at the clock on her mantelpiece. It read 10:00 a.m. Keery felt positively indulgent. She made herself a trencher of cheese and bread and poured a large glass of ale. Tucking in, she enjoyed a leisurely meal by the fire. No knock at the door disturbed her while she swept and dusted her little cottage. She even made it to evening mass. It wasn't until four the next morning that a knock disturbed her rest. Birgitta Hoskin was in labor. She and her husband, Tobias, lived in the manse, the largest home in town. Tobias was a merchant. Keery was lucky to have been chosen to be Birgitta's midwife. The fussy young mother required a lot of attention, which meant Keery was called to the manse for frequent visits. Each visit added more coins to her meager stash. Keery was not greedy by any means, yet she dreamed of delicate curtains adorning her little kitchen window, softening the glow of streaming sunlight.

Birgitta was buxom and well-built for childbearing. Though it was her first baby, her labor was rapid. Her body just seemed to know exactly what to do. It was ready to send baby number one into the world and prepare itself for birthing the next nine that would surely come. Birgitta's baby was crowning within an hour. When her hands touched the blood-stained head of the child, Keery felt something she had never felt before. The terror of a thousand souls ran through her in one split second. Another push from Birgitta and the child was born, and Keery's vision gone. The child would not suffer, she knew, but would cause great suffering. It was a boy lying limply in her hands with the umbilical cord wrapped around his neck. Keery's throat tightened. What should she do? The child had not yet drawn breath. She could let him expire. She could save many from suffering, were her vision to be trusted. It would be easy to say he had been born dead. He had the cord wrapped around his neck. Birgitta was anxiously peering at the midwife and baby through her spread knees.

"Is he all right?" Birgitta asked. Keery looked up at the question and saw in the mother's eyes fear and love for her baby. She looked back down at the limp body, bluish around the lips. He was a perfect baby otherwise. Sweet, like all newborn babies. Without further thought, Keery loosened the cord and coaxed breath into the baby's lungs. Soon, he let out a mighty wail. Keery handed him over to his waiting mother. Stoically, Keery finished the rest of her duties, waiting for the placenta, cleaning and clearing things away, and packing her bag. She left a happy mother with a nursing child as she slipped out of the manse.

Once again, Keery was plagued by the fear that she had done the wrong thing by letting a child live. When she arrived home, she did not unpack her things for her customary cleaning. Instead, she knelt before the little altar in her living room. The statue of the Virgin Mother, wearing robes of robin's egg blue and a gilt crown, had been her one indulgence. It had made a deep gouge in her savings. She prayed to it now, her heart pouring out her fears before the saintly young mother depicted in wood. Was she wrong to allow such suffering into the world if she could stop it? Was Luanne right? Was the purpose of the gift of sight for snuffing out suffering? She looked up at the statue, its beatific eyes staring perpetually up to the heavens. She would get no answer here. Keery looked at her hands. They had helped usher many lives into the world already. She wouldn't use them to usher it out. Perhaps she would answer for it one day. She prayed the virginal lady would speak up for her when the time came. A knock at the door caught her attention. She sighed and stood. It was Peony.

"Astrid's water broke," the young woman told her.

"Tell her I'll be right there."

* * *

This story first appeared in the After Dinner Conversation—April 2023 issue.

Discussion Questions

1. Would you be willing to work as a midwife if it meant seeing the future of the child being born?

2. Should any baby be put to death under any foreseeable future? Is there any situation where killing the newborn is the right choice?

3. In the story, Keery hesitates in her decision to allow the birth of a child who will live to cause misery for others. More so than when she decided to allow a child to be born into experiencing a lifetime of misery. Do you agree with this distinction?

4. Would it be better to tell the parents of the child's future so they could choose whether the child lives or dies? What are the pros and cons of this approach?

5. What, if anything, is a practical distinction between killing a child in the story and terminating a pregnancy in modern society when a severe genetic defect is found?

* * *

E v e n i n g S t a r

E. B. Ratcliffe

* * *

Content Disclosure: Strong Language; Graphic Violence; Suicidal Themes; Depiction of Homophobia

* * *

A red streak of light flashed across the curtains. Robert grimaced and Grace got up to look out the window. There were two police cars pulling into the parking lot and it had started to snow again. She turned around. Robert was kneeling on the bed. He'd grabbed the gun and was watching her.

She held out her hands to him. "Robert, I didn't tell anyone where you were."

Robert nodded his head and sat back against the pillows. The gun was cradled in his lap. "I know."

* * *

The snow fell like lace streamers in the dim afternoon light. The school's chain-link fence had two big oaks standing sentinel just outside the school grounds. Everything was shrouded in white. From inside the classroom, the school's window framed the snowy scene as if a play was about to begin.

The class was studying *A Portrait of the Artist as a Young Man*. Grace liked Joyce. His words poured over the reader. Words held power. Even the word *snow* held power. Malleable and as flexible as any word could be. Inuit natives built single-word discussions on the base word of snow. They could have a million combinations to describe snow, a million ways for snow to infiltrate their thoughts.

Three boys in jackets and baggy jeans stood outside the fence. Snow collected on their shoulders and caps. The flare of their cigarettes blinked on and off like fireflies. Grace wished she were out there with them. They'd text, trade jokes, and try to keep warm.

"Miss Ki, are you working on the midterm assignment?"

Grace turned her attention to Mrs. Combs at the front of the class. "Yes, ma'am. I like to organize my ideas in my head."

"Who are you working with?"

"Robert Lascor." Robert looked up from his paper and nodded. Mrs. Combs shrugged. "Carry on."

Several of the other students were staring at Grace. Emily Sims scowled her disapproval. Emily was the easiest to read of the popular kids. Since Grace had gotten a buzz cut, Emily worked at getting under her skin. She posted online that Grace was a dyke. It wasn't true. She liked boys. Robert liked boys too. They'd spent hours discussing boys, even though neither of them had yet to have sex with one.

Sex was a word that had at least fifty derivations in English. They could do a midterm on sex as a base word for the English language. She rubbed her temples. There was a literary discussion that wasn't going to make it to midterms.

If not sex, perhaps love could work. In English, love was an overused and diluted word. Like fuck; it held no power. In Greek, the words for love were powerful and descriptive. *Eros* meant passionate love and *filia* brotherly love. *Agape* was the word for a bigger love, a love of humanity, an unconditional love in the spiritual sense. Grace looked around at the students hunched over their desks. She wanted them to wake up and see that there was something there, *agape* waited.

English used agape for leaving something totally open and ajar. Mouths are left agape in amazement, wonder, and fear. She liked that. It could be a midterm. She liked the idea that the greatest and purest form of love the Greeks defined was somehow related to something left open. Love was found in the open, like the sky. Open, like when a person's mind and heart were not closed, when people put them at risk, when people conquered fear, *agape* was there.

She stared again out the window, the snow appeared out of a vast gray expanse of nothing. It was a magician's trick. She was open to love, open to change. Grace looked forward to college, but it no longer dominated her thoughts. Now, she'd rather grab up Robert. Get him away from his parents. She hated them even more than her own. They'd go to LA and get tech jobs at some start-up, maybe. It would absolutely send her mother off the deep end. Mom's love was not *agape*. Mom's love was boundaries and control.

Robert frantically scrawled on and on into his notebook. He wasn't tapping into a tablet like everyone else in the class. His head bobbed and his long blond hair bounced as if he'd heard the hoofbeats from the four horsemen of the Apocalypse. Grace chewed one of her fingernails. Literary allusions of love would not satisfy Robert. He would want something more real and yet so much less. He wasn't feeling the moment sliding past, the snow calling to them in its chilled whisper. Instead, on the page, his pencil scratched short staccato bursts in counterpoint to the ticking fingernails of everyone else.

Grace pushed her glasses back up the bridge of her nose and watched the storm intensify. Snow blotted out anything beyond the fence. She was alone in her admiration. Everyone else was writing, getting a head start, missing out on this minute that stretched into infinity.

The bell rang and Robert swiveled in his seat. His blue eyes alight, he plopped the page torn from his notebook down in front of her. She scanned the white page, stopping about halfway down, and focused on the prose.

"Is this about last summer with the gray sky and closed door?" Grace asked.

Robert pointed to the bottom of the sheet.

She rubbed her hand against the stubble at the back of her head. It read like a short play. Robert's memory open for their classmates' icy derision. Not going to happen.

Picking up her backpack and Robert's torn page, Grace stood up. "Let's get out of here."

Grace marched him over to an alcove by her locker. "Are you serious? You want to come out in front of the whole class."

Setting his books down by his feet, Robert rolled his eyes and pulled out his phone. "They already know. It couldn't get worse?"

Stupid. It could get worse. Their uptight insulated prep school wasn't safe.

Grace held up the page. "Robert, what about your dad?"

Looking up, Robert shrugged. "Reverend King said the truth will set you free. Dad'll have to cope."

"Like he did last summer?"

Putting his phone back into his pocket, Robert crossed his arms. "He won't do that again. He promised. He's an ass, but he sticks to his word." Robert leaned in and rubbed her arm with his hand. "I got to be myself some time."

Grace tapped the paper with her chewed fingernail. He had a point. He had a good sense of humor. People liked him. It might prove better protection to be the school's gay poster boy. "Promise me that if our most excellent and trustworthy peers get out of line, you'll let me know."

Robert smiled and held up his three fingers. "Scout's honor."

"Shit. You aren't a scout."

"Used to be."

Grace grabbed his hand. They didn't have much time before the next bell. Some of the more empathetic kids might watch out for him. Grace glanced up just in time to see the Neanderthal jock Danny plunk a finger against the back of Robert's skull. "Hey, dykes."

After Emily's post, the popular kids branded them both with this hilarious new nickname. Defiance had its price. Robert was pretty with his long hair and kept getting mistaken for a girl. Robert winked at her and twisted around giving Danny a sultry stare. "I heard you'd like a menage with some lesbians. How 'bout it?"

Danny's posse laughed as he scowled and retreated. Tennis shoes smacked the tiled floor in a diminishing beat.

Yeah, Robert was definitely liked well enough to have this work. Why not? If this worked, great. If not, she'd personally put her classmates in a snowy grave under one of those oaks.

* * *

Grace and Robert spent two weeks rehearsing his paean to last summer. They polished the presentation until it was flawless. Still, it didn't stop Grace's stomach from clenching up at the midterm. Robert might run away again if the class hated it. He couldn't make it on the street. She never should have agreed to this. Grace wiped her sweaty hands on the back of her red jeans. She'd dressed up for the performance in a white blouse with a bra underneath, not that she needed it all that much. Grace braced herself for things to go wrong. Come watch the freak show. A few of the girls had laughed when they'd pulled the teacher's desk over against the windows. It didn't matter. Those girls would have laughed at anything involving her.

The day was winter bright with sun shining through the frosted glass. Gone was the snow and its protection. Grace's feet hurt a little from her new combat boots, but she'd done enough acting not to show it. She'd rehearsed Robert's piece so many times that she could have recited it backward standing on her head. It was time to do it.

Robert, dressed from head to toe in black, sat on a chair to Grace's right. She took a deep breath. She was damned if she'd mess up Robert's true confession. Grace checked out the fifteen other students. Most of them sat back lounging, bored, and ready to hate anything they did. A rebellious thought ricocheted in her head. You monsters are about to get stomped. A thrill of adrenaline ran giggling up her spine. She spoke low in a voice that would resonate to the back of the room. "The moon shot through a web of stars into the presence of despair."

She pressed her hand out toward Robert. "Body crumpled on the floor like dirty laundry with no feeling. The apartment was old with matted carpets and faded drapes. He had found it in the summer after he escaped from his parents."

A few of the boys in the class sat up straighter and Emily grinned. Robert's disappearance at the end of junior year hadn't gone unnoticed. He'd ghosted everyone, even her. Nobody knew what happened when he came back, but Grace.

She could see Robert's tortured smile out of the corner of her eye as he began speaking. "He couldn't look into his parents' disappointed eyes. Their angry lips pressed together. He escaped, sixteen-year-old and best boy, for the sweet relief of a man's regard."

Nobody looked surprised. Nobody cracked a nasty remark. The tension in her legs and arms fell away. The only person it really mattered to was Robert and he'd done it. He'd come out to the whole school, no going back now.

Grace had the next line and she stepped in a little closer to Robert. "Narrow butt pushed into the floor. Dishes left from yesterday. In the window, a gray August sky. And the door, the closed door..."

They turned their heads in perfect synchronicity and focused on the classroom door before Robert spoke. "...the door cutting off the air."

Grace wanted to look trapped. With bent knees and turned-out feet, she paced. Rattling and spitting out the words as though they could break her out of there. "He didn't move. The clock continued ticking, a fly buzzed around his face, and an alarm went off somewhere."

She began spinning. Keeping it slow and steady. "The clock sat next to the bed, ticking in its wind-up fashion, and soon it's going to..."

She froze with her arms up as Robert screamed, "Stop!"

The class was paying attention now. Grace spoke. "The moon shot through the web of stars into the conscious presence of bright death."

Grace pounded on desks in the front row. She pounded with the fury she felt. Robert couldn't even get a frigging job at McDonald's without his parents' permission; those same people who beat him and tossed him out like garbage.

She wailed at the smug faces in front of her. All these teenagers adored by their parents. "Coins were scattered on the dresser next to a small framed picture of a boy at a junior high school graduation."

Grace stopped drumming on the desks and Robert hugged himself before saying, "He smiled for the camera held by his father."

She walked over to Robert. "He ran out of money and was being evicted."

Abandoned in that distant city. Mocked at school and all alone. Alone. Grace touched a lock of his blonde hair. "He collapsed onto the floor to the right of the bathroom."

Pulling confetti from her pockets, Grace began throwing it out over the class. Garish circles of paper floating down, catching the bright sunlight. "That small bathroom, with drops of red glistening on the peeling walls."

Robert stood. Pulled up his sleeves. Pink scars on his wrists held out to the class. Hoarse voice whispering, Robert dropped to his knees. "His body crumpled on the floor. Only he could see the blood."

All the jerks who called him names must be so proud of themselves. You left those scars. Grace spoke softly. "His eyes stared without knowing emotion. His tears had fled in anger hours before. The pain in his mind was gone. The decision was made."

Robert crawled to the chalkboard, turned around, and said in a soft voice, "He pushed numbers on his cell's screen. Three rings and an answer."

Robert lay on the floor, cradling his head in his arms. "Dad, come take me home."

Grace stared at her classmates. She managed to get her clogged voice to speak. "The moon shot through the web of stars into the conscious presence of another corpse and the moon forgave."

* * *

After school, Grace worked on homework at the kitchen table. Physics was driving her crazy this semester. She heard Mom and a man's voice in the front room but hadn't a clue what they were talking about. Why couldn't Grace remember whether the small p was density or pressure? It was like another language. Looking up as her mother stomped in, Grace could see she was in trouble. Mom waved a couple of typed pages at her like a matador. "You told that class you're a lesbian. What is wrong with you?"

English class. Grace clenched her fists watching her knuckles turn white. Mom always got it wrong. "I'm not gay."

"Your teacher called Robert's parents. God, Grace. His parents were furious."

An electrical jolt went through her. "Did his dad hurt him?"

Mom threw the crumpled pages onto the table. "Don't be ridiculous. His father was just here. He got copies from your English teacher."

Mom wiped her palms against her khaki slacks as though they were dirty. Grace stared down at the ruined script. "What did he do to Robert?"

"Nothing. He took away his phone and burned his journals. Lord knows what else the boy wrote about. He ran off again."

All Grace felt was a cold rage at Robert's father. It wasn't enough to have Robert at the crevasse of despair. He had to kick him into it. "Shit! Goddamn him."

"Grace, I don't want to hear that kind of language."

Standing up, Grace pleaded for her mom's understanding. "He might as well have killed him. Robert was only living through this by writing."

"Sit down. You sit back down and talk to me in a civil tone."

Grace slammed down onto the kitchen chair. Her mind jittered through what Mom had said. Where was Robert? She pinched at a corner of his script. Grace couldn't even text him.

Mom spoke in an earnest tone. "Robert's parents are worried about him. No one wants their child to be homosexual. You can see that. They want him to live a healthy life. This kind of public thing could destroy his future."

Grace counted to ten. She wanted to sound reasonable. "He's gay. It's what he is. They need to get over it."

Mom let out a big sigh and pulled on her fingers. Her

voice was dark with disapproval. "I understand better what his parents are going through. I could never get over you. His father was almost in tears just now he was so worried."

"Worried? He's the one hurting him."

"Oh, like Robert has no part in it." Mom pointed down at the script. "Grace, this paper. What that boy's doing, it is just a phase."

Mom was hopeless. Grace stood up. "I need to go find Robert."

Reaching out quickly, Mom dug her fingers into Grace's arm. "No."

Grace jerked her arm away. "Give me one good reason why not?"

Mom stepped into her space like a wrestler. Her breath was warm on Grace's face, the smell of mint gum and cigarettes. "Robert took his father's gun. The police are looking for him."

Robert never told her about a gun. She needed to find Robert. She needed to get out of there. Grace whispered, "Robert wouldn't shoot anyone."

"I won't risk your life on that. Do you know where he is?"

Grace trembled with anger. She straightened and looked into Mom's eyes. "No."

"You're lying. Go to your room. I'm calling your father."

The *Nightmare Before Christmas* ringtone on Mom's phone made them both jump. Her mother pointed an admonishing finger at Grace to stay put and brought it to her ear.

* * *

Grace snatched the keys off the kitchen counter and ran. Mom raced into the yard as she cranked the car around at the end of the driveway, but Grace floored it.

She turned left onto Sheridan Avenue and drove toward school. Robert might head for school. No. He wouldn't. She gripped the steering wheel hard to hold herself in place. Nervous energy was shooting up and down her arms. He'd look for a private place.

She wiped at her nose with the back of her hand. Grace had to hold it together better than this. Jesus, it was cold. She could see her breath. She wished she'd had time to grab her coat. Grace flipped the blinker on with a touch of her thumb and drove onto the interstate headed east. The heater began to warm up the air a bit, but not enough. She was shaking.

Robert didn't drive. He wasn't in a car, so he'd bus it. He didn't even have his cell. She couldn't text him. The dilapidated motel renting by the hour on Santa Fe Boulevard? She took the exit onto I-25, a faster route. Cutting class, they'd spied on the sex workers in their natural environment. Robert called the motel "Elsie" after the song in Cabaret. The motel Elsie was the happiest corpse they'd ever seen.

Warm air was finally blowing out and Grace stretched her fingers into the heat. Would Robert use another name when he checked in? A cop car followed her off the highway. Damn Robert's parents to hell. She let out a held breath when the police turned north.

Grace headed onto a street with a crowded gray industrial park. Desolate concrete darkening under the waning sunlight, all the snow gone. The motel, Poolside Manor, was five blocks down on the left. A neon sign missing most of its letters blinked Po--side—an. The god of oceans, exiled to a Colorado motel, hundreds of miles from water.

* * *

Grace's muscles still jittered when she parked the car. It was like she was on some major caffeine jag. Please, God, let him be here.

Grace worried that the unshaven desk clerk would be a problem, but he didn't even look up from his phone. "I'm looking for a young blond guy. Robert?"

"Room 103."

It was that simple. Her pulse picked up and everything took on a sharper edge. Get there. Get there. Get there. The warmth of the car wore off. Hugging herself, Grace raced along the cracked sidewalk. At her knock, half of Robert's face peeked out from some hideous orange and brown curtains.

"Grace?"

"Robert, let me in. I'm freezing."

"You shouldn't be here."

She looked up and down the strip of deserted sidewalk. "Robert, let me in, please."

The door opened and he looked blond, tired, and sad. Grace hugged him and pushed him back into the room. "Jesus, it's cold out there. Are you okay?"

It was dim in the dingy room with only one lamp. There was a pause. Robert moved past her and shut the door. "No."

Grace rubbed her hands up and down her arms for warmth. "Your parents called the police."

He lifted an eyebrow at her and walked over to the bed. "Yeah. They're prostrate with worry. How'd you find me?"

She followed him over to the bed. The gun was sitting on top of the bible next to the phone. Grace couldn't get to it without knocking him over, so she'd have to reason with him. Not her forte. "Elsie. Predictable."

He sat down and smoothed the neon green bedspread with his hand. "To you."

"Yeah, but what's up with Elsie? Why would she wear curtains that ugly?"

It wasn't that funny, but he laughed and pulled himself all the way onto the bed.

"You're wrong. Bad color schemes suit Elsie."

Grace sat down at the foot of the bed. "No. We could fix her up. Sew her some new curtains."

He pushed back a strand of hair from his cheek. The lamp made his hair look like spun gold.

Robert looked at his hands. "Home economics."

"Vogue patterns."

Her heart pounded in her ears as she waited for his answer. Please, please, give her some time. He almost smiled. "Are you always this good at ruining a perfectly good sulk?"

"Give your parents another chance. My mom said your dad almost bawled."

He pulled his knees to his chest and wrapped his arms around them. Stupid. She shouldn't have mentioned his dad.

"He fuckin' hates me, Grace. Ransacked my room. Took my phone. Burned my stuff." Robert ran his sleeve across his face. "Dad said *they tried*. Want me out."

"Assholes."

"Yeah. My Uncle Bill, the marine, will take me to San Diego. Make me a man."

Grace rubbed her combat boots together, mashing down the old shag carpeting. "So we'll get away together."

"I don't want to feel this way anymore."

Grace could feel her throat closing up. She was on the

verge of a major crying jag. No. Damn it. She'd lose him.

Robert scooted up to her and put his hand on Grace's shoulder. The waterworks went on full blast. She pushed her face into his shoulder and Robert held her as she cried. Grace finally pushed back and looked at him. "Long day. Why don't we take the car and get out of here?"

A red streak of light flashed across the curtains. Robert grimaced and Grace got up to look out the window. There were two police cars pulling into the parking lot and it had started to snow again. She turned around. Robert was kneeling on the bed. He'd grabbed the gun and was watching her.

She held out her hands to him. "Robert, I didn't tell anyone where you were."

Robert nodded his head and sat back against the pillows. The gun was cradled in his lap. "I know."

Grace went to the door and shoved the security chain into its lock. She was thinking maybe they could get out through the bathroom window when she heard the blast of the gun. Her ears rang and the smell of gunpowder was overpowering.

Grace leaned against the door. She could feel vibrations of someone pounding on it. She turned and Robert was slumped against the headboard. Blood sprayed behind him and gushed out over his chin.

A horrible animal scream ripped out of her throat as she ran over to the bed.

His blue eyes were empty above the gaping mouth. Grace picked up the gun from the bed. She sat down next to his body as the door splintered open. A large policeman crashed into the room.

"Boy, put down the gun. Robert, put it down," he yelled at

her.

Robert was dead. Why was the policeman talking to him? Then she realized that he'd gotten them confused. He thought Robert was the girl and she was the boy.

Grace felt agape, open wide and empty. She felt as if she was enveloped in the falling snow. God, she envied Robert. Maybe she'd been wrong. She held the gun up higher so the policeman could see she hadn't fired it. The cop made a guttural sound. She thought that he should use his words. Words held power.

* * *

This story first appeared in the After Dinner Conversation—November 2021 issue.

Discussion Questions

1. Should Robert have came out to the school or unhappily waited it out until he could move out of the house and live his own life? Why do you think he couldn't simply wait a bit longer?

2. Let's get into the mind of Robert's parents. Why do you think they were so offended by having a gay son? Was their real goal not to have a gay son, or not to have a gay son people knew about? Did they simply not think they might lose their son forever?

3. What (*if anything*) should Grace have done differently in this story and why?

4. Why did Robert feel suicide was his only option? What would you have said to him in the hotel room if you had been Grace?

5. What happens next in Grace's story? What does her relationship with her parents look like after this? What is her plan for the next few years?

* * *

Author Information

Corporate Head

Jacob Orlando is a queer young man of letters from small-town Texas now based in Boston. He works a day job and writes away his free time. *www.jacoborlando.com*

Eleven Things I Have Left Now That My Daughter Is Gone

Vickie Fang is a former lawyer who did volunteer work with prostituted women in Baltimore for nearly ten years. She is working on a collection of short stories inspired by these women and has also just revised a Baltimore lawyer thriller. She is a big fan of classical Chinese poetry and is finishing a novel set in eighth-century China in the immediate aftermath of the An Lushan rebellion. She publishes a Substack of poetry translations. *https://chinesepoetry.substack.com*

On Ice

Laura Mullen has been published as a regular contributor to *The New York Times* and was accepted to the 2024 Northern California Writer's Retreat. She sits on the board of the literary arts organization Pittsburgh Arts & Lectures, and is currently seeking representation for her debut novel, *Missing Eden*. She lives in Pittsburgh with her husband and three young children. Instagram *@lauramullenwrites*

Junk

Taylor Lawritson is a teacher and writer of fiction originally from Glendale, Arizona. They currently live in Prague, Czech Republic, where they spend their time writing about gender, society, and the unreality of modern life. This is their first piece published in a literary magazine. Instagram *@thesauruscollector91*

Disconnect

Julia Meinwald is a writer of fiction and musical theatre and a gracious loser at a wide variety of board games She has stories published or forthcoming in *Bayou Magazine, Vol 1. Brooklyn, West Trade Review, VIBE,* and *The Iowa Review,* among others. Her work as a composer has been heard in productions across the US and in Canada, and the cast album for her musical *The Magnificent Seven* streams on various platforms. *www.juliameinwaldwrites.com*; *https://linktr.ee/juliameinwald*

Emancipation

Darcy Alvey worked as a freelance journalist and editor-in-chief of a regional Southern California magazine, winning several national writing awards given by the North American Mature Publishers Association. She now concentrates on writing short stories, her first love. She has had stories published in *Wilderness House Literary Review, Foundling Review, The Write Room, Waypoints* and more. She believes the Oxford comma lends clarity.

Lies I Tell My Father

J.G. Alderburke once won a T-shirt in a writing contest sponsored by a beer company. Other wins include having stories appear in *The Saturday Evening Post, Hawai`i Pacific Review, White Wall Review,* and others.

Q-tip Options

Steve Parker retired and pursued his passion for writing. He is now a graduate student at Kennesaw State University. After years of enjoying literature as a reader, he recently took up the pen to share his own thoughts and experiences. With his debut article, Steve offers a unique perspective on life and its intricacies. His engaging storytelling and profound insights captivate readers, leaving them with a newfound appreciation for the beauty of small, everyday moments. The question of free will is central to much of his work.

Visions of Midwives

C.S. Griffel teaches English and creative writing at a small university in central Texas. Besides short stories, she writes screenplays and is learning to love poetry. Her stories also appear in the *William and Mary Review* and *Talon Review*. She is also published in *I Found Happiness and Tragedy: Selections from the 2022 Literary Taxidermy Competition*.

Evening Star

E. B. Ratcliffe has lived in the Northwest with his husband, Joe, for over twenty years. Inspired by the loss of a gay high school friend, "Evening Star" is set in Denver where he grew up and went to college. "Evening Star" was originally written and produced as a one-act play in Seattle. His first book, *Yellow Finch*, was a finalist with the Pacific Northwest Writers Association. He is grateful to *After Dinner Conversation* for bringing this story to life again.

Additional Titles

After Dinner Conversation - *Technology Ethics*

After Dinner Conversation - *Crimes & Punishments*

After Dinner Conversation - *Bioethics*

After Dinner Conversation - *Nature of Reality*

After Dinner Conversation - *Equality Ethics*

After Dinner Conversation - *Research Ethics*

After Dinner Conversation - *Government Ethics*

After Dinner Conversation - *Business Ethics*

After Dinner Conversation - *Examining the Past*

After Dinner Conversation – *Food Ethics*

After Dinner Conversation – *Sex & Sexuality Ethics*

After Dinner Conversation – *Interpersonal Ethics*

After Dinner Conversation – *Interpersonal Ethics*

After Dinner Conversation – *Philosophy of Religion*

Or subscribe to our monthly print/digital magazine.
www.afterdinnerconversation.com

Additional Information

Reviews

If you enjoyed reading these stories, please consider doing an online review. It's only a few seconds of your time, but it is very important in continuing the series. Good reviews mean higher rankings. Higher rankings mean more sales and a greater ability to release stories.

Print Books

https://www.afterdinnerconversation.com

Purchase our growing collection of print anthologies, "Best of," and themed print book collections. Available from our website, online bookstores, and by order from your local bookstore.

Podcast Discussions/Audiobooks

https://www.afterdinnerconversation.com/podcastlinks

Listen to our podcast discussions and audiobooks of After Dinner Conversation short stories on Apple, Spotify, or wherever podcasts are played. Or, if you prefer, watch the podcasts on our YouTube channel or download the .mp3 file directly from our website.

Patreon

https://www.patreon.com/afterdinnerconversation

Get early access to short stories and ad-free podcasts. New supporters also get a free digital copy of the anthology *After Dinner Conversation–Season One*. Support us on Patreon!

Book Clubs/Classrooms

https://www.afterdinnerconversation.com/book-club-downloads

After Dinner Conversation supports book clubs! Receive free short stories for your book club to read and discuss!

Social

Connect with us on Facebook, YouTube, Instagram, Bluesky, TikTok, Substack, and X (Twitter).